Taming Jake

by

JoMarie DeGioia

PUBLISHED BY:

Bailey Park Publishing

Taming Jake

Book Two of the
Cypress Corners Series

by

JoMarie DeGioia

Chapter 1

Chapman Financial, Boston

"Pick a lane."

Jake Chapman turned from the wide window framing the gray fall day to face his father across the plush office. "What?"

"Pick a lane, damn it," Bill Chapman said.

Jake shook his head. "Who's Elaine?"

Bill slammed the door and stalked closer. "A lane, Jake. Make a decision for once in your life."

Jake swallowed a grin. This again. He settled into the big leather chair behind the desk and placed his hands behind his head. As he toyed with the small gold ring on his left earlobe, he watched his father's face turn red.

"Is this about grad school?" he asked.

Bill threw up his hands, wrinkling the sleeves of his expensive suit jacket. "Yes, it's about grad school. It's about work. It's about everything, for Christ's sake. You never finish anything."

Jake shrugged. "So I only work at Chapman Financial a few months out of the year. What do you care? I bring in more money with my projects than any other exec."

"It's not about…" Bill's gaze slid to one corner of the room as his words trailed off.

"Ha! Don't say it's not about the money, Dad." Jake straightened, placing his palms flat on the desk. "It's always about the money and you know it."

Jake thought he saw a flicker of something in the old man's eyes, gone in an instant. It had to be nothing. Bill Chapman didn't do emotion and even he admitted to worshipping at the altar of the almighty dollar.

"Look." Bill took a breath and blew it out. "You're almost thirty. School isn't doing it for you. Chapman obviously isn't doing it for you. You need to decide what you want."

"Why?"

Bill looked as perplexed with Jake's question as Jake was with his statement. Why pick a lane, as his father put it? He should make a choice and then live with the consequences? No friggin' way.

Bill settled across from him and wiped his hand over his face. His father was built like both Jake and his brother Rick. Tall and broad and athletic. The years had been good to Bill, too. Years Jake and his siblings had been without their mother while Bill dedicated his every waking moment to making money.

Jake could read his father and knew the conversation would soon turn. He folded his hands as he waited and fingered a callous on his thumb, the result of the past weekend's climb upstate. Another challenge, another rush. Maybe it was time to try something new. He'd been at Chapman for two months now, and that was about as long as he could stand being cooped up in an office.

"I want you to go to Cypress," Bill said.

"Cypress?" Jake felt the familiar tingle of anticipation go through him. "The courses are a go?"

Bill nodded. Jake had pitched his idea to the investors last month, detailing his plan for adventure trails in the middle of a wild, lush property set in Central Florida. Cypress Corners—pricey homes, championship golf course and secluded resort—was the perfect setting for his "Adventure Excursions." Bike trails, rock walls, lake obstacles, rope bridges. The place would have it all and bring in a ton of money for the developers and

Chapman Financial's investors.

As part of the deal Jake would be the one to design it, then he would test it so that the out-of-shape executives it was made for wouldn't hurt themselves while they enjoyed their managed thrills and careful excitement. But man, would Jake have a blast testing it himself. To its, and his, limits.

"The investors gave it a go," Bill said. "And they agree that you're the one to spearhead the project. God knows you can use some direction over the next couple of months setting it up."

Jake ignored that last dig and took the faith of the investors at face value. "They won't regret it. And I'll get to see Rick and his family."

Bill's lips thinned but he said nothing. Jake's big brother Rick hadn't talked to the old man for almost four years now. Not since he told Bill to take his job at Chapman and shove it. Bill should be relieved in that respect. At least Rick had made a choice.

Rick and his wife Harmony lived in Cypress Corners with their son, and Jake couldn't wait to see them again. Jake wouldn't let Rick's choice to stay out of the family business drive a wedge between the brothers.

Jake stood. "When do you want me there?"

***

Cypress Corners, Florida

Claire Callahan's fingers danced over the keyboard as the numbers popped onto the screen in front of her. The budget, the input of numbers that represented more money than she'd ever touch in her lifetime, was her responsibility. She gladly took it on. She was always the responsible one. The one who stayed the course, took the steady road. It had brought her the CPA controller position at Cypress Corners at the age of twenty-six. It paid her a salary that let her put a steady amount toward her student loans and still put aside enough to gain some security in her life. Security she sorely craved.

Another Friday afternoon drew to a close. Some of the offices around her were already dark, their occupants off to start their weekends a little early. Claire didn't begrudge them. At least they had something to do. Somewhere to go.

"Hey, are you still here?"

Claire turned to nod at Tammy. Tammy was one of

the sales reps for the property, and she was all smiles and promises. Truth be told, she was also one of the reasons Claire had such big numbers to input. While separate custom builders and contractors worked on the property, the development itself earned a hefty percentage on land and home sales.

"Yes," Claire answered. "I don't want this waiting for me on Monday."

Tammy tossed her head in answer, her shining black hair sliding over one shoulder of her expensive silk blouse. Claire knew the cost of things, since she had to balance her personal budget down to the penny. She'd like to be able to wear clothes like Tammy's, but as much of her salary as she could manage went directly into her savings.

"Well, I'm off to the beach." Tammy grinned. "Love this time of year. No kids around."

Claire just smiled. Tammy took off, bound for her little convertible and her escape less than an hour away to the east. As for Claire, she'd had enough of the beach when she'd lived with her family on the east coast of Florida. It might still be pretty but it held more bad memories than good. So there was no escape for Claire.

An hour later, Claire shut down the computer and stood. She stretched her arms toward the coffered ceiling and let out a groan. She had to allow that her office was decorated beautifully, a nod to the developers who made Cypress Corners the successful project it was. Claire lived right here at Cypress too, in a modest house nestled in one of the more densely-populated villages that dotted the sprawling property. It was a two-bedroom bungalow with deep moldings and hardwood floors and the bare minimum of furniture.

"Hey, Claire."

Claire picked up her bag and turned. Rick Chapman, Sales Director for Cypress, looked at her expectantly.

"Hi, Rick." She snapped off the light and shut her office door. "I'm surprised to see you back here."

Rick shrugged and gave her that handsome grin of his. He held up a soda can. "Harmony wanted a diet cola with lime and we're out at home."

Claire smiled. "Harmony's a woman with very specific wants."

Rick laughed. "Yeah. Good thing she still wants

me."

Claire couldn't be surprised at that, really. He was gorgeous, big and strong and clearly devoted to his wife. And he was just as lucky to have her friend Harmony in his life.

Rick walked beside her as she left the building for the small parking lot set beside it. She listened to the sand crunch beneath their feet, ticking off the seconds before he made his move. She knew he'd ask. He'd asked every day this week despite her continued refusal. Tonight he waited until she reached her car.

"Are you coming on Sunday?"

Claire's shoulders slumped. The barbeque. It's all he and Harmony had talked about all week, and always conspicuously within her earshot. She had only her Sunday free, as usual. Tomorrow she'd be tied up with Cally like she was every Saturday. Her father took all of her energy on their days together. That was for sure. But Sunday? Oh, what the heck. What was she going to do instead? Stay in and watch movies on Lifetime?

"Yes, I'm coming. What do you want me to bring?"

Rick's smile widened.

***

Sunday couldn't have come quickly enough for
Claire. Yesterday Cally had been alternately pouty and
cheerful. Something was definitely up with her father.
She'd taken him out and they'd shared a meal at their
favorite hotdog stand, and she'd listened as he'd
reminisced about her mom and the life they had before
she died five years ago. If only their life had really been
as Cally described it. She'd worry about him later,
though. God knew he would still be there later. He
always was.

Rick and Harmony's house faced the lakeside park,
and was wrapped by a wide brick porch which held
wicker furniture and wooden rockers. Claire felt the
tension of Saturday evaporate as she climbed the few
steps up to the front door. She could hear a child's
laughter from behind the house, and the sound was light
and sweet and carried on the temperate breeze. Her belly
clenched, as it always did when she thought of the child
she'd love to have. Someday.

She shifted the plastic box in her hands and rapped
on the wooden frame of the screen door.

"Hey!" Harmony held the screen door open for Claire. "I'm so glad you could make it. Come in, come in."

Claire's friend had her curly golden hair up in a ponytail, looking half her age as a smile curved her lips. Claire felt a tingle of apprehension mixing with the happiness at seeing her friend. Uh oh. She'd seen that smile before. Harmony was up to something.

"Rick didn't make it easy to keep saying no," Claire said.

She handed Harmony the container of home-baked cookies. Baking was one of Claire's few escapes. She bought ingredients in bulk and searched out new recipes to try. Following the recipes to the letter and presenting the perfect treats gave her a useful application of the math she adored.

Harmony lifted the box to peer through the plastic. She gave a little moan. "God, I love your chocolate-chocolate chip."

Claire smiled at the compliment and followed her into the house. Pitchers of iced tea and lemonade along with plastic cups were set on the granite counter closest to the French doors leading out to the patio. Harmony stole a cookie before setting the box beside a plastic tray of obviously store-bought brightly-colored and heavily-frosted cupcakes.

Claire regarded the supermarket treats. "What's with all the sugar?"

Harmony shook her head. "Those are Rick's brother's idea of the perfect treat for a three-year old boy. If Nick eats one of those I'll never get him to sleep tonight."

Claire honed in on one thing Harmony said. Rick's brother was here. The elusive Jake she'd heard about. Thrill-seeking, globe-hopping Jake Chapman. Claire now knew what Harmony's smile had meant. She smelled a set up. Wasn't that just great?

There was a gilt-framed mirror hanging beside the French doors, and Claire couldn't resist taking a quick glance in it as she went outside. She was no Tammy, but she was no slouch, either. Her strawberry-blond hair was thick and wavy, her skin clear if dotted with more than a few freckles. She looked tired, though. And certainly not as young as Harmony did even though Claire was a few years younger. Oh, well.

She stepped out onto the patio and froze as she glimpsed the finest butt she'd seen in a long time. With a strong back above and long legs beneath, this guy had a body Claire could look at for hours. He wore his dark hair a little long but it looked thick and glossy.

"Jake!" Harmony called.

The guy straightened and turned. Claire's belly clenched again. God. He was a god! The tan on his face and a dusting of dark stubble on his square jaw made his blue eyes sparkle like the small gold hoop in his left ear. Ooh, he looked like a sexy pirate. He was tall like his brother, but Jake Chapman was a bit leaner, his muscles more defined beneath his soft-looking t-shirt. Claire stumbled over her Keds as she stepped off the patio onto the grass.

"Hey, watch out," Jake said. He picked up a large toy truck on the grass right in front of her, one of several parked on the lawn. "Nick's got himself a whole fleet out here."

Claire swallowed as he stepped closer and held out his hand.

16

"I'm Jake."

She shook his hand and quickly released it. His touch was perfect. Firm and warm and sure. He smelled fresh and hot, like a day at the lake on a summer afternoon.

"Claire Callahan," she managed to say.

His brows shot up. "You're Claire?"

Was that disappointment in his voice? Or interest? Claire wasn't going to try to guess right now.

"Rick and Harmony told me about you." Jake winked. "You're the money mind of Cypress."

She inwardly winced. God, how boring that sounded.

"Yeah," she said, forcing a smile. "That's me."

She turned and sat on a lawn chair. Any second now the hot Jake Chapman would turn his attention from the boring "money mind."

"Lemonade, Claire?" Harmony asked from inside.

"Yes, thanks."

Jake stared at her a little longer, and Claire shifted uncomfortably. She fingered the collar of her pretty embroidered camp shirt, an end-of-season splurge she'd picked up at the outlet center in Orlando. She crossed her legs, and her khaki shorts suddenly felt a little too short as he dropped his gaze slowly to her feet. Then Jake let out a shout as Nick grabbed his legs from behind.

Jake tumbled to the grass, reaching behind to catch his nephew to his chest. He hugged the little boy, and the two of them laughed as they rolled around on the lawn. That was the sound Claire had heard before. It was light and irresistible and made her stomach flip.

She took the glass of lemonade Harmony handed her and traced her fingers over the condensation dripping down the sides. She watched Jake and Nick. This guy was a thrill seeker? A risk taker? Right now he looked like a stable family man, but that couldn't be right. She eyed his perfect profile and model hair. Maybe an advertiser's idea of a stable family man, then.

She took a long sip of the tart, sweet drink as her mind worked around the puzzle of Jake Chapman. She was a smart girl. There wasn't a puzzle she couldn't decipher.

She hid a real smile behind her glass.

Chapter 2

Jake watched Claire out of the corner of his eye. Harmony hadn't been exaggerating. The girl was very pretty. He noticed she did everything with precision too, down to the even stripe of mustard down the center of her hotdog. He piled chopped onions and poured ketchup onto the big fat burger Rick grilled him, then smashed a bun onto the juicy mess. He took a bite. Mmm, he could still taste the charcoal. He loved his brother's cooking.

Nick had finally given him a rest, and now played quietly on the grass as he digested the hotdog he'd wolfed down. Emotion came over him like a wave. God, he loved that kid. Rick was damn lucky he'd come here to Cypress four years ago. He found the love and family he never got from Bill and got the hell away from Chapman Financial.

The afternoon waned, and their pool beckoned. He flicked his eyes over at Claire, taking her in with a sideways glance. Had the CPA brought her bikini? Jake doubted it. She didn't seem like the bikini type. It was a damn shame, too. She really had a nice body. With full, round breasts under that cute pineapple shirt. Smoothly-

19

muscled legs leading up to a sweet butt wrapped in khaki shorts.

She wasn't much taller than Harmony, maybe five four if he had to guess. She'd pulled all that luscious hair up into a ponytail at some point, leaving little ringlets teasing her cheeks and the nape of her neck.

Her face was heart-shaped, and her crystal blue eyes were something else. And God, she had freckles. Yeah, she had freckles to go with that strawberry hair. He had no choice but to face it. Claire Callahan was cute. He looked at her legs as she shifted on the bench. Yeah, she was cute. And more than a little hot.

Jake rested his arms on the picnic table and leaned in toward where Claire sat across from him.

"So how long have you worked at Cypress, Claire?"

She faced him fully then, her eyes wide, and he felt it straight to his gut.

"Seven months," she said.

He nodded vaguely. That would explain why he'd never seen her before. He would have noticed if she'd been around the last time he was here right after the New Year.

"Coffee?" Harmony asked him.

Jake nodded again and took the mug she gave him and watched as she snapped open the tray of cupcakes he'd bought, her lip curled. Suddenly Nick appeared to snatch the biggest, gooiest one and took a bite. The kid grinned, bright blue frosting smeared on his nose and chin, and Jake chuckled.

Harmony rolled her eyes at Jake. "If he stays up all night he's going in your room."

Jake laughed louder and dipped his finger into the neon green icing on another cupcake. He licked off the icing and noticed Claire watching him. Her lips parted and he could see her little pink tongue. Damn. The jolt to his midsection began to spiral downward.

He nudged the tray toward her. "Cupcake?"

She blinked, then shook her head. "No, I don't really like that type of frosting."

"You have to try the cookies Claire brought, Jake," Harmony said.

Jake looked at the plastic box Harmony set in front of him. Dark, rich chocolate chips dotted a couple dozen cookies just a shade lighter. The cookies were perfectly

round, and each one was identical to the one beside it.
Beneath it. On top of it. He breathed in, detecting a hint
of cinnamon.

"Wow, these look great." He looked at Claire. "Did
you get these at the bakery in the village?"

"No," Claire said. "I made them."

"You made them?" He picked up two of the cookies
and held them side by side. "But they're all exactly the
same."

Claire's cheeks turned pink and she fiddled with the
stack of napkins in front of her. "So?"

He looked at the cookies lined up in the box and
winked at her. "Is there the same number of chips in each
one?"

She shrugged. "Nearly."

He hid his grin. Man, she was pretty when she
blushed. He took a bite of one of the cookies. Who cared
what they looked like? They were the sweetest,
crunchiest cookies he'd ever tasted.

"Mmm." He licked a crumb from his lip.
"Unbelievable."

A smile broke across her face and the blow to his gut

moved lower still.

"Thanks," she said.

He grabbed another cookie. Claire took one for herself, nibbling around the perimeter until all that was left was a bite-sized piece she popped into her mouth. She'd eaten her hotdog in even bites, too. Did she eat like that when she was really hungry? Or would she give in to the urge and indulge her appetite if the mood struck?

Twenty minutes later Jake watched her as she stood and walked over to Harmony. The setting sun turned her hair to fire and her skin all rosy. She moved with grace as she said her good-byes and leaned down to ruffle Nick's hair. Jake grabbed another cookie and took a bite.

Claire Callahan. He savored the rich chocolate taste. These cookies were incredible. And so was the baker. And with a body like hers, it would be a shame if she restrained all her appetites.

***

Claire let herself into her house and placed the foil-covered dish on the counter. It held one of Nick's cupcakes, which Harmony had insisted she take. It didn't appeal to her. It had too many sprinkles and too much frosting. Mmm, frosting. After Jake had licked the frosting off his finger a drop had lingered on the corner of his well-formed mouth. She'd had the urge to lick it off. The thought sent a tingle through her now.

"Stop it, Claire," she muttered. "He probably thinks you're nuts."

He'd been obviously unimpressed with her work at Cypress. He was bored in the very least. He'd remarked about her cookies, too. Yes, she made certain every single one was perfect. She'd been teased about that before. That was for sure. He'd watched her eat, though. Very closely. His expression told her he thought she was doing something strange with the methodical way she ate. So she wasn't comfortable just diving into everything like he seemed to be. She never was and she never would be.

She thought of that dab of icing on Jake's lips and felt another tingle in her belly. Reaching out a finger, she touched the pink cream dotting the cupcake. She pulled back but not before a drop decorated the tip of her finger. Unable to resist, she licked it and shuddered.

She turned away from the cupcake and the naughty

thoughts it provoked and wiped her fingers on the folded dishtowel set near her sink. Glancing at the phone on the counter, she checked for messages. She kept the landline because she believed in having backups. What if her cell battery was down? What if she lost her phone, which even she admitted was highly unlikely? She was relieved to find no light flashing. There was no call from Cally, then. Thank God. Yesterday had been trying enough.

Her father, Joseph "Cally" Callahan, had been fidgety when she'd paid her weekly visit yesterday. The mobile home she'd secured for him in a snug fifty-five plus community in nearby St. Cloud six months ago was comfortably furnished, and just big enough for a single man with no responsibilities. No responsibilities. That was Cally to a T. He suffered from macular degeneration in his right eye, but his happy-go-lucky personality never seemed to falter. He held court there more often than not, in the recreational room or outside on the shuffleboard and bocce courts. Charm was his gift and he had it in abundance. It was what made him a successful car salesman back in the day and what made her mother believe every empty promise he made them. He'd told her time and again that you had to believe what you said to make the sale, and she knew he believed every puff of smoke he'd blown in her mother's eyes.

Yes, yesterday he'd seemed restless during her visit. Oh, he was full of the usual stories. She'd had to listen for the hundredth time to the tale of the big win fifteen years ago, that time at the track when his pick had rushed over the finish line first against the odds. Claire shuddered as the memory struck her now, her hands clenched at her sides. The odds weren't usually a friend to her father.

They'd lived high on the money he'd won that time, Cally, Claire and her mother. For nearly a month they'd been able to afford new clothes and dinners out. Toys and books for Claire. Jewelry for her mother. And then the money had disappeared. Like it always did. His commissions on the cars he sold and his bonuses for being salesman of the month time and again. It all disappeared.

Claire's stomach churned and she pushed the memory aside as she turned to the fridge. She opened it and grabbed a diet soda. No lime, no lemon. Just store-brand diet cola in a plain red can.

She opened the soda and took a sip as she settled onto the couch. The furniture in her place was bought at a bargain, too. From a big box, close-out store not far from Cypress Corners. Her couch was covered in linen that was easily washable. It was very practical. It was also soft and comfy and hers. Her TV wasn't as large as some they sold now, but it was a Black Friday steal last year. She had no use for the HD channels, though. She wouldn't pay for more than the basic channels right now. But it was a Sunday night in October, and the networks had some good first-run episodes on tonight.

Tomorrow her work week began again. She took another sip of her soda. Maybe having limited free time wasn't such a bad thing. She wouldn't have the luxury of worrying much about Cally during the coming week. Not about his odd mood this weekend, anyway. Her gaze strayed to the cupcake. And she wouldn't be tempted to day dream about Jake Chapman, either. She closed her eyes and leaned her head against the back of the couch.

But wouldn't it be nice to have a few day dreams for once in her life?

***

The next morning Claire sat at her desk. She was one of the first to arrive at Cypress as usual. She hadn't slept well, but at least her commute was short. And her workspace was ready and waiting for her.

Her pens stood neatly in their holder on her desk and she grabbed one out of habit. Her inbox was empty. Her outbox was filled from the work she'd finished Friday night. She booted up her computer and waited for the programs to load, tapping the pen against the desktop as she did so.

She picked up her double-shot latte to go, her one and only indulgence. The coffee shop in the village made the strongest brew, and she brought the cup to her lips. The steam tickled her nose and just the thought of caffeine sent her nerves springing to life. She parted her lips and tipped the cup. And burned her top lip.

"Hot!" She put the cup down and held a napkin against her lip. "Darn." She sucked in a breath. "Every darn morning."

Much more slowly this time, she drank some of her latte. It was creamy and rich, and just what she needed.

"Morning!" Tammy called as she stopped in Claire's doorway. "What a weekend." She leaned into the office. "What did you do?"

"Nothing special." Claire put the cup down again and turned to face Tammy. "Did you have a nice time at the beach?"

Tammy grinned. "Very. You should come with me next time."

Claire shook her head. "I couldn't. I have— I couldn't."

Tammy shrugged. "The offer stands, Claire. Any weekend you're free we can head out to Melbourne and have some fun. Oh!" She spun on her heels and looked down the hall. "Is that…? Oh my God, it is." She hurried in that direction, leaving Claire gaping after her.

Curious, Claire stood and crossed to the doorway. She heard a voice then, the rough rumbling she'd come to recognize as one of the developers of Cypress. It was accompanied by another deep voice. Oh, Claire knew that voice, too. That tingle went through her again. Darn.

Turning, she started to close her door.

"Claire?" her boss's voice called.

She closed her eyes. Darn, again. "Yes, Mr. Forbes?"

"Come out here for a minute, Claire. There's someone I'd like you to meet."

Straightening her shoulders, she pulled the door open again and walked down the short hallway to the sales lobby. She was right. Jake Chapman stood with his back toward her, dressed in well-fitting chinos and a dark blue polo. He turned when Mr. Forbes gestured toward her.

"Jake, I want you to meet Claire Callahan." The developer's smile flashed from beneath his neat salt-and-pepper moustache. "She's the one who keeps our books in order."

Jake ran his gaze over her and her tasteful sage-green suit from last season. She tried not to fidget but she couldn't help feeling a little dowdy next to Tammy's up-to-the-minute polish. And why was Tammy standing so close to Jake anyway?

"We've met," Jake said. His eyes sparkled. "We had dinner together yesterday."

Tammy's eyebrows arched in surprise, then she turned toward Claire. "Nothing special, Claire?" she teased.

Claire waved Tammy's question aside as her cheeks heated. "It's nice to see you again, Jake."

It was really nice to see him, if she were being honest with herself. The softly-tailored clothes looked as good on him as his shorts and T-shirt had yesterday. His hair was smoother today, but a few loose strands of it fell forward against one cheek. And that stubble was still evident on his chiseled cheeks, as was his fresh hot smell.

"Jake here is going to bring more money into Cypress, Claire," Mr. Forbes said. "So be prepared to balance a lot more numbers."

Pulling her gaze from Jake's twinkling pirate's eyes, Claire focused on her boss. "It's what I do, Mr. Forbes."

Mr. Forbes smiled. "I know I can count on you."

The corny joke wasn't one of his newest but Claire gave a soft laugh anyway.

Tammy grabbed on to Jake's arm. "Tell me all about this new venture, Jake. I'll need to add it to my sales pitch."

Claire watched as Tammy's fingers stroked his bare arm. She wasn't jealous. She had no reason to be. But

31

still.

"I was just going to show Mr. Forbes the plans for the courses and trails."

Jake caught Claire's eye and grinned, obviously pretty pleased with himself. She couldn't help smiling in response.

"Why don't you two join us?" Jake asked.

Tammy let out a little squeak. "Definitely. If it's anything like you told me the last time you were here, it should be incredible."

Tammy's words struck Claire. *The last time he was here?*

"Join us, Claire?" Jake asked again.

Jake's enthusiasm was contagious, and she didn't doubt his presentation would be captivating. She looked at Tammy again, at the way she leaned toward Jake. Tammy needed to hear Jake's proposal now, not her. Tammy was the one who had to sell clients and potential buyers on the development and the upcoming amenities. Claire had no true reason to sit in on the meeting. She had no excuse to watch his eyes sparkle as he laid out his plans, either.

She shook her head. "I'm sorry, but I can't."

Was that disappointment on Jake's face for a split second? Not likely. As for Mr. Forbes, he just nodded.

"Go to those numbers then, Claire," he said.

The developer turned away, already escorting Jake and Tammy to his office. He'd come to expect Claire to spend her day stuck in her chair, glued to her computer. And whose fault was that?

Ignoring the sound of Tammy's chatter, she went back into her office and closed the door.

Chapter 3

Jake looked at Claire over his shoulder as he walked away. She was still standing in the hallway, her hands clasped in front of her. He'd seen the interest in her eyes when he'd invited her to come along. But now her mouth was set, her luscious lips thinned to a line.

"Tell me about the endurance run, Jake." Tammy still had her hand on his arm. She gave him a squeeze. "How long can you last?"

Jake rolled his eyes. God. Did Forbes get what she was clearly talking about? Jake had been tempted to take Tammy up on her offer the first time he'd come to Cypress. But there was something frightening about her. Sure the sex would have been mind-blowing but he had the feeling she'd have his balls in a vice the next morning. No thanks. Now she probably thought he was a challenge. That was just great.

"I'll show you," he said, making sure to include Forbes in the statement.

He pulled away from her and stepped to the other side of Forbes' office where the secretary had put his plans. He went through the printed renderings as he began an abbreviated version of his vision. He'd scheduled a meeting with the key investors for the next week, during which he would get into the details including the proposed rates and fees for participants. As for today, he was simply laying out the plans for the ambitious courses.

"The courses will take the best and most challenging aspects of Old Florida—deep lakes, rolling terrain, thick brush—and shape it into fitness trails that will be both safe and demanding," Jake began. "The rock walls we'll construct on the natural sandy trails will challenge our clients to push themselves to the limit, as will the rope bridges high over the lake."

Forbes and Tammy leaned forward in their chairs as he continued. By the time Jake was finished describing the first trails to be constructed, Tammy no longer had candlelight and satin sheets in her eyes. No. Dollar signs were there now. That was precisely the response he wanted from everyone connected to the property. That way they'd leave him to make his vision a reality with as little interference as possible.

"What about the lakes?" Tammy asked.

"Swimming in the lakes." He flashed a smile. "We'll regularly check for alligators. Add running and biking on the wilderness trails, and we'll give clients the feel of participating in a triathlon."

"My God, it'll be fantastic," Forbes said. "They'll be pumped and want to spend their downtime, and their money, in the restaurants and clubs in the village."

Jake nodded. "That's what the investors are hoping for."

"Has Rick seen these plans?" Forbes asked.

"Oh, yeah." Jake grinned now. "Until he's sick of them."

"Excellent." The developer nodded and stood, signaling the end of the demonstration.

"Thank you for your time, Mr. Forbes," Jake said.

"Any time, Jake. And keep in touch."

Jake knew that the simple words meant Forbes wanted to be informed of all contractors under consideration. So much for a lack of interference. But if Bill had taught Jake anything, and there wasn't much Bill had taught any of them, it was how to keep the money men happy.

36

"Certainly." Jake grabbed up his materials and waved Tammy ahead of him out of the office. "I should know more about the contractors' bids by next Friday."

Jake followed Tammy out into the hall and turned toward the doorway he thought was Claire's. He saw her name on a brass plate beside the door and smiled. The door was open and she was transfixed by the computer screen in front of her. She'd taken off her green jacket and it hung over the back of her chair. Her high-heeled shoes were set precisely on the floor to the side of her desk, and her legs looked silky-smooth in hose nearly the color of her skin. She had delicate feet tucked beneath her desk chair. With high arches and pink-painted toenails.

"Hey, Claire," he said.

She started and turned. He caught her quick intake of breath, the way her beige shirt parted slightly, and he caught a glimpse of pink lace covering her breasts. Interesting.

"Hi, Jake."

Her voice was all breathy. That did it.

"Come to dinner with me tonight?"

Claire stared at him for a beat, then swiveled in her chair to face him fully. "Dinner?"

"Yes, dinner." He flashed a grin at her. "With me."

Her eyes widened and he was secretly pleased he'd caught her off her guard. He guessed he'd startled her when he'd stopped at her door, too.

"Tonight?" she asked, her voice a squeak.

He stepped into the office, which suddenly seemed much too small. He could smell her scent in here. Something like vanilla but richer. Mmm.

"I thought we could hit the Clubhouse," he said.

She worried the hem of her skirt, which made it ride up just a bit on her thighs. The silence continued for a bit too long. What was she thinking about?

"Claire?"

She caught Jake's eye and his chest hitched.

"Take a chance for once, Claire," she murmured. "Sure, Jake," she said, her voice much clearer now. "I'll have dinner with you."

For the first time he was at a loss for words. Take a chance? What, she never dated? Or was it him, what he was, that put her on her guard? He pushed aside that

38

thought.

"Great. I'll pick you up at seven."

"I'll meet you there," she rushed out.

He started to object, then just nodded. "Okay. See you then."

As he turned he watched her swivel quickly back around to face her computer.

Maybe tonight he'd get her to keep her focus on him for longer than two minutes. Although with those big blue eyes of hers, he was afraid of what she'd see if she looked too closely.

***

The Clubhouse was just as Claire remembered it. She'd eaten at the pricey restaurant at the golf course only once before, right after she was hired, and on the developers' account. The place was way out of her budget but so elegantly comfortable. The candlelight, the clink of glasses, the fine linen tablecloths all spoke of easy luxury.

From the way the girl at the hostess station greeted Jake, he'd obviously been there before and more than once. Claire got a less enthusiastic greeting herself. She

couldn't really blame the hostess. Jake looked too good
to ignore tonight, even for the few seconds it would take
to acknowledge his dinner companion.

He wore a gray suit jacket over a blue knit shirt, both
topping charcoal chinos that fit his butt quite nicely.
Even his hair looked neater tonight. And that little gold
hoop winked as it caught a bit of the ambient lighting.

He waved her ahead of him and Claire could feel his
eyes on her as she passed him. For a moment she felt she
looked as good as any other woman here. Her dress
might be from last season but it was washed silk, with
shades of blue and green brushed over the fabric. She'd
found the strappy sandals she wore at the end of the
summer, but the leather was fine and the height of the
heels was comfortable yet a little bit sexy. She figured
she looked as good as she possibly could on her budget.

She saw that there was hardly an empty table in the
place. And on a Monday night. Even when Cally was
flush the family had never gone out to eat on a
weeknight.

The hostess escorted them to a table near the wide
windows that framed the rolling hills of the golf course

beyond. The course at Cypress was award-winning and busy throughout the year. And now that the heat of the summer was almost passed, it and the development would experience a surge of business. She couldn't help but feel a touch of relief at the sense of job security the sight of the full restaurant gave her.

"Please tell the wine steward to bring us a bottle of Pinot Grigio?" Jake said to the girl. "Is that okay, Claire?" he asked her.

Claire simply nodded. Jake held her chair for her and as she sat the back of his knuckles brushed her shoulder blades. She stifled a shiver. Who could blame her? The silk dress was pretty thin. And his fingers were pretty warm.

"Thanks," Jake said to the hostess. He removed his jacket and slung it over the back of his chair. He pushed up his sleeves as he sat across from Claire, she couldn't help watching the play of muscles beneath his knit shirt. She lifted her gaze and found him watching her.

"I like that dress," he said.

She fiddled with her napkin-wrapped silverware. "Thank you."

As his eyes strayed down the front of her, she could feel her nipples tighten beneath her lacy bra. She stifled a shiver. Was the air conditioner blowing overhead?

His mouth tilted up at one side and she stiffened. He couldn't see through her dress. And certainly not through the lacy bra she bought at the twice-yearly clearance sale at Victoria's Secret!

"You look hot," he said.

So much for the AC. With his eyes on her she felt like she was burning up. Darn her pale skin anyway. There was no hiding her blush from him.

Thankfully the steward arrived at their table right then, with an open bottle of wine and two glasses. The steward poured a splash into one glass and handed it to Jake. Jake took a sip, closing his eyes as he rolled it around in his mouth. A drop was on his full lower lip and Claire licked her own. He opened his eyes and nodded to the steward who poured out two glasses and left the bottle. Jake raised his glass to Claire and she felt compelled to do likewise.

"To a dinner without trucks and sticky fingers," he said.

"Or cupcakes."

Jake shrugged. "I don't know. That frosting was pretty tasty."

She smiled and took a cautious sip of the expensive wine. It was delicious, woody with a touch of fruit. He watched her as he drank, his eyes glittering over the rim of his glass. He lowered his glass to the table and picked up a menu. He handed it to her before taking his own. Wow. The chair, the wine, the menu. The guy was pretty gallant for someone who spent his time bungee-jumping off bridges. A gentleman and a daredevil. It was a startling combination.

"What do you feel like tonight, Claire?" he asked.

She wouldn't focus on those hands holding the menu, Those fingers when he lifted one hand to his ear and fiddled with his earring as he considered his own selections. That sculpted chest outlined beneath his finely-woven shirt. She forced her attention on the menu. The place was very pricey. She swallowed and forced herself to make a choice.

"I guess I'll have the crab cake and a field green salad," she said. *Twenty-four dollars.*

"That's it?" His eyebrows arched. "Why don't you try the—"

"I'm good, Jake." Her smile felt forced this time. "Thank you."

He shrugged and opened his mouth to say something but their server came to the table. He gave the guy Claire's order. "I'll have the rib eye," Jake said. "Medium rare."

Forty dollars.

"And a Caesar salad, I guess," he added. "Oh, and bring some of your crawfish chowder." He glanced at Claire with a small smile. "Two bowls."

Ten dollars a bowl. "Jake, I don't need soup."

"It's my favorite, Claire," he said. "And I won't be comfortable eating when you have nothing in front of you."

She thanked him again. She'd have to return the favor somehow, but there was no way she could afford to take him to dinner here in repayment. Maybe she'd make him a batch of white chocolate macadamia cookies. Those were the most expensive treats she made per cookie.

"So you've been at Cypress for seven months." Jake took another sip of his wine. "What did you do before?"

"Studied, mostly. Earned my CPA license," she answered. "It was a long road."

Jake raised his brows in surprise, then nodded. "I know. I still haven't finished my graduate studies."

He was a scholar, too? Did the man have any flaws?

"What are you studying?" she asked.

He laughed, but it wasn't as easy a sound as he'd made earlier. "Everything and nothing."

"But what is your discipline?"

He crossed his arms and leaned toward her. "I'm not a big one for discipline."

His smile was a little crooked on one side. There was that charm again. Claire felt it straight down to her belly. She took another sip of wine.

Their chowder arrived and she savored every bite. She caught Jake's eye and returned his smile. "It's delicious. Thank you."

The rest of the meal was as good as the beginning. With just the soup and the crab cake in her stomach, the wine had a heady effect on her. Candlelight, soft music and Jake Chapman. How could she feel sleepy and tingly at the same time?

He talked about everything and nothing, just as he'd described his graduate studies. Finances and obstacle courses, quarterly returns and rock-climbing. He spoke of traveling where the road took him and dropping in at Chapman Financial to make a few bucks before taking off again. He was completely rudderless.

Being a person as focused as Claire has had to be her whole life, she couldn't imagine not having a course to steer by. Focusing on where she put each foot before taking a step was all that kept her going the past few years.

Jake settled the bill. Claire didn't dare look at it but she had a pretty good idea he'd dropped close to two hundred dollars on their meal. Then they stepped out into the quiet gardens set to one side of the Clubhouse. The evening was a little cool but, although it was the beginning of October, true autumn was weeks away.

As they walked for a bit, Claire tried to put numbers out of her mind. What Jake was thinking of, she couldn't guess. She thought once more about what he'd said about his graduate studies.

"But where do your interests truly lie?" she had to know.

Jake's eyes rounded in surprise. "I'm interested in a lot of things, Claire." He led her over to one of the sculpted benches that dotted the walk, this one looked like a butterfly, and they sat. "Why settle for one road when there are so many?"

"I couldn't be that easy," she said.

He leaned close, and the moonlight slashed across his face. Her heart began to pound. He was almost beautiful.

"Where do your interests lie, Claire?" he asked. "What is it you want?"

Claire swallowed and mirrored his pose, turning toward him on the bench. She was a breath away from him and stared into his eyes.

"I want a stable, simple life," she admitted.

Jake suddenly pulled back and laughed. "Simple? Stable? Ah, Claire." He winked at her and grabbed her hand. "You should try my course when it's finished."

Fear slammed through her in an instant. "Oh, I

couldn't."

"The rush," he said. "The thrill of the unknown. God, it's incredible."

The thrill of the unknown? She'd lived with that her whole life. She knew it then. They didn't stand a chance at anything more than a fling. She just wasn't a fling type of girl.

But for just a second, she wished she was.

Chapter 4

Jake closed his laptop and unplugged it.

"You know, you're welcome to stay here while you work on the project," Rick said.

Jake shook his head. "No way, bro. You and Harmony have enough on your plates without a permanent guest."

"Ha!" Rick crossed his arms. "When have you ever been a permanent anything?"

Jake just shrugged off his brother's question and slid his notes into their large folder. "Harmony's tent-cabin is perfect for me. It's wired and has a bathroom. A kitchenette."

"You're romanticizing it, Jake. It's primitive."

Jake zipped the folder shut and straightened. "I've slept under the stars on the side of a mountain, Rick. That tame campsite is perfect for me."

Rick didn't argue the point but Jake knew his brother just wanted him to stay close for longer than a few weeks.

"I can pretty much only make coffee out there. I'll show up here to eat whenever you want me."

Rick grinned. "Good."

Jake's eyes pricked and he turned back to his duffel bag. "Have you heard from Cassie?"

Their wild-child little sister was a subject they often danced around. Neither Jake nor Rick had steady contact with their father but they both knew Cassie used her connections to the Chapman money as often as she could.

"Last I heard she was in Monte Carlo."

Jake groaned. "God. Expect a call for an extension of credit, Bill."

"And he's stupid enough to give her more money to play with."

Jake nodded. He and Rick had their father's number and had little to do with him. Cassie? She used him like her personal bank and, for some reason, Bill let her.

He zipped the duffle closed. "Tell Harmony I'll see her at the Institute tomorrow afternoon."

"Yeah, the tree-huggers have to sign off on your plans."

Jake knew Rick didn't mean anything negative about the Institute or their vision. True, it was Harmony's vision but Rick was fully on board. Of course, he no longer had to butt heads with his pretty plant angel now that she was his wife. Jake, on the other hand, had to dance to their tune and prove that what he was proposing would have no negative impact on the environment.

Cypress Corners was very different where pricey developments were concerned. Championship golf course, boutiques and shops and custom homes were bracketed by conservation areas set aside for native plants and wildlife. Seventy percent was set aside, to be exact. It was different, but Jake loved the wild parts of Cypress much more than the civilized parts of the village. And moving out to Harmony's tent-cabin was just what he needed.

"So will you have any company out at that tame campsite?"

Jake caught his brother's eye. "Of the female variety, you mean? I don't see how."

Rick's brows raised. "I thought you went out to dinner with Claire on Monday night."

Jake nodded. "I did. I thought we hit it off, too. Then she got all distant and... I don't know. Cold isn't the right word but something happened."

Rick looked thoughtful for a minute. "I know she has trouble letting herself go. Harmony's always trying to get her to loosen up but the girl is focused."

"On her job. Yeah, I get it." Jake zipped the duffel closed and shouldered it. "Oh, well. It is what it is."

Rick snorted. "Whatever that means."

It was Jake's turn to grin. "Hey, I go with the flow. You know that."

"Just don't get lost out there. Our little man loves his uncle."

Jake assured him he would keep in touch, then went outside and climbed into his Jeep.

The campsite was on the far lakeshore. The area was starting to be developed for recreation but it was far less utilized than the main lake area. That suited Jake just fine. It would afford him privacy and the quiet to fine-tune his proposal. As he bounced over the sandy terrain, he thought about that stilted conversation with Claire at the end of their date two days ago.

She'd been so sweet and open while they'd shared their meal, although it was clear she kept an eye on the prices of every single item on the menu. Then again, she was a bean counter. Numbers were her gig. That was for sure. But later, when he'd gone on about the thrill of the unknown she'd grown shuttered. Maybe he'd laid it on a little thick, but he'd been trying to impress her. Going on and on about the road less traveled or some load of crap.

"I'm an idiot," he muttered.

He'd seen her at the Sales Center just yesterday but they hadn't done more than nod a greeting at each other. It was just as well, since Tammy had him in a stranglehold and all but dragged him to see the latest model rendering of the development. He planned to add to it and soon, so he'd managed to put Claire and her quick-change act out of his mind. Today after lunch at the Clubhouse, he'd looked for her but the door of her office had been closed tight.

Whatever the reason she'd turned cold on him Monday night, he knew he and Claire just didn't connect. That didn't make any real sense, since he'd felt the sparks at Rick and Harmony's and during dinner. Had he been wrong? No. He'd felt the heat between them. The fact that he still found her incredibly hot was apparently just beside the point.

Stopping in front of the tent-cabin, he shut off the engine and pulled the brake with a creak. Moving himself in wouldn't take much time, which was good because he had to review his notes for his presentation to the Institute. His first presentation, of course. They had to be informed of every step along the way, from planning through construction and implementation.

Jake stood and stared out at the pristine lake stretching out beyond the cabin. The trails he would create would be far more elaborate in scope than anything he'd designed at the other resorts Chapman investors had their hands in. Even the ones at the Aspen property paled by comparison. That particular course, completed last winter, was featured in several outdoor sports magazines, which brought more visitors and more money. These trails at Cypress would engage residents and visitors along with corporate partners eager to schedule retreats for their tired and overworked executives. All while keeping the spirit of the wilderness and Old Florida alive and well.

He entered the cabin and flicked on the light. The place was sparsely furnished but he didn't mind. It was clean and neat and just what he needed for the time-being. There were a few homey touches, left behind by Harmony. A soft quilt she'd told him her mother made covered the mattress of the iron bed, and there was a thick rag rug spread over the plank floor. He hadn't been messing with Rick when he'd told him he'd slept on the side of a mountain with virtually no shelter. This would be far better. Besides, he wouldn't be here that long.

The period leading up to the construction would probably be the longest, leaving the installation of the prefabricated climbing walls and other apparatus until shortly before the test runs. He figured maybe just over three months to get to that point. He thought about spending the holidays at Cypress with Rick and his family last year and knew he wanted that again. So win-win, in his opinion.

He stashed his clothes in the small dresser beside the bed, placed his few toiletries on the shelf nearest the back door and crossed to the kitchenette. He hadn't been kidding when he said he'd just about make coffee out there on his own. The two-burner stovetop and small microwave would suit him, as would the frat-boy fridge.

He cracked it open, smiling when he saw the bottles of beer inside.

"Thanks, big brother," he said, grabbing a cold one.

He twisted off the top and stepped out onto the wooden porch facing the lake. Taking a long draw, he thought about his upcoming presentation. He had to be cool. Concise. He had to get his points across with enthusiasm and expertise. The folks at the Institute weren't messing around, and he couldn't either.

He sat down in one of the two Adirondack chairs and leaned back, letting out a breath. The sun was low behind him now, the pinks and oranges winking off the placid ripples on the surface of the lake. The Cypress trees dripped Spanish moss toward the water and the insects hummed in the dying warmth. This place was beautiful and Jake totally got the whole tree-hugging thing even if it had taken his brother falling in love with Harmony to see it.

Their father never would, of course. Conservation and appreciation for nature was just a way to build the portfolio. No matter. Jake was pleased to his bones that he could create a project here that would celebrate this beauty and also kick ass. He took another drink of his beer and closed his eyes.

He just hoped he could pull this off.

***

Claire rinsed her dish and set it in the dishwasher, then wiped down her counters. Today had been nothing out of the ordinary, which she usually relished. Routine and the expected was her home base. But today she'd felt like something was missing. Yesterday she'd caught a glimpse of Jake at the Sales Center, but he'd been wrapped up in Tammy. About the adventure excursion courses, she knew. Just how long would it be before they were both wrapped up in each other, though? What was it to her, really? She'd had one date with Jake. That was all.

Then today she'd thought it was Jake's voice she'd heard in the reception area but she'd stubbornly kept herself in her office. She wouldn't go running out there like some teenage fan girl or something.

Speaking of Tammy, she'd told Claire that Jake was getting ready for his presentation to the Institute on Friday. The sales staff wouldn't be in attendance, not that Claire would be invited to sit in either. Her involvement would come later. When the project passed this hurtle and came back around to logistics and costs. Sheesh, that even sounded boring to her tonight.

"I'm not going to stick around here," she said, brushing her hair back from her face. "Pining after hot Jake Chapman like I have nothing else to occupy myself."

She didn't have much, but she had something. She'd go into St. Cloud tonight and shoot a few games of pool. True, she never went there midweek. When she went, it was usually on a Friday night. Still, it would get her out of the house and maybe she'd make a few dollars in the process. She could count on the guys at the End Zone sports bar for a stress-free evening. Some friendly competition, maybe some harmless flirting, and she'd feel more centered. More at home.

She dressed in jeans and a T-shirt, then drove her Prius the ten miles into St. Cloud to the End Zone and pulled into a parking space. It was only seven o'clock on a Wednesday night, but a lot of the spaces were taken up. Mostly with big trucks and motorcycles, which wasn't unusual for the rural town. Her Prius wasn't the only hybrid vehicle parked here either, though. Shouldering her purse, she stepped up onto the sidewalk and entered the sports bar.

The End Zone was a little dim inside but the large dining room to the right was lined all around with TVs set high on the walls broadcasting fishing shows and Ultimate Fighting matches along with other sports. The scent of French fries and buffalo wings hung in the air, along with the ever-present malty beer smell. There were families seated at a few of the wooden tables and booths. Couples, too. A long bar stretched along the back wall and the wait staff buzzed around with round trays of food and drink. Some country pop song was playing on the digital juke box and the crack of cue against ball could be heard as she neared the wide opening toward the room to the left.

"Hey, Claire," Beth, one of the servers said. Her blond ponytail swung back and forth as she wiped down the bar. "Surprised to see you on a Wednesday."

Claire shrugged. "I felt like getting out of Cypress."

Beth laughed. "Stepford a little too perfect for you?"

She'd heard the development called that by the

59

locals before and just smiled. "Maybe." She tilted her
chin toward one of the banners blanketing the high wall
behind the bar showcasing a seasonal ale. "A hard cider,
please."

Beth handed her an open bottle of the apple ale and
Claire paid her and took a sip. Crisp. Cool. Tangy.
Perfect for a fall evening. Turning, she headed into the
pool room.

A few games were going on, and there were about
six guys and half as many girls scattered around four of
the six tables. The two closest tables were open.

"Hey, Claire," Mark called as he walked toward her.
"You're here on a Wednesday?"

Claire swallowed a sigh. Was she really so
predictable? She knew the answer. Yep.

She took another sip of her ale. "Yes, and I'm ready
for a couple of games. You in?"

Mark grinned. "Five bucks a game?" She nodded
and he leaned on his cue. "Rack 'em."

She took up the triangular rack and began to gather
the balls on the nearest table. Mark was in his mid-
twenties and cute in a cowboy sort of way, with wavy

brown hair, big brown eyes and a cleft in his chin. They'd teased and flirted a little over the past few months but it didn't seem like either one of them was looking for more. She racked the balls and stood back, waving him to break.

Mark leaned over the table and took his breaking shot, then stood. "So what brings you here on a Wednesday?"

"I just wanted to get out tonight," she answered, watching the balls as they knocked around the table.

He'd pocketed the yellow striped so she was solids. He took another shot and sank the number eleven. He was good, but she was better. All she needed was for him to miss a darn shot and this table would be hers.

"You seeing anyone out there in Stepford?" Mark asked with a wink as the number fourteen went into a pocket.

"Funny. Cypress isn't that perfect, Mark."

He shrugged and effortlessly sank another striped. "Too prissy for me, thanks. And you didn't answer my question."

No, she hadn't. She wasn't going to, either.

"Don't you need to concentrate?" she asked instead.

He smiled again and took another shot. And missed, thank goodness. She didn't bother hiding her smile as he stepped back to yield her the table.

"Look at miss cocky."

"Not cocky, my friend. Confident."

Mark apparently had no argument to that. She sized up the table, taking in the angles and cushions and pockets as she leaned her head to one side. She eyed the balls, his and hers, on the felt and it came to her with the familiar pop. She knew what shot she had to take and leaned over the table. With a satisfying crack, the cue ball struck the number five and sank it right where she'd planned.

In short order, she sank all the solids but the eight ball. She called out the balls and pockets as she did so, something she knew could be a little cocky which is why she did it in this particular game. Mark deserved it for that Stepford remark.

"Eight ball, right corner," she said, bending over to make the last shot of the game.

The crack as the cue ball struck the black ball was

one of her favorite sounds when it was her stick doing the work. The eight ball rolled smoothly over the felt to sink gracefully into the indicated pocket and she slowly straightened.

Mark cursed softly behind her and she turned. She arched a brow and he chuckled.

"I owe you five, Claire."

She smiled now and took another drink of her ale. "You better keep count, because we're just getting started."

Chapter 5

Friday dawned and Jake was up before the sun. His presentation to the Cypress Institute wasn't until eleven o'clock, but he wanted to go over his notes. And then go over them again.

As he pored over the sketches he marveled that he'd never stressed over a presentation like he was over this one. Maybe it was because this one had a much larger scope. Maybe it was because Cypress was his brother's home. And maybe, just maybe, it was because he wanted to prove to his father that he could "pick a lane" and take a real direction.

He traced one finger over a more strenuous route through the courses that included the high rope bridge. "I'll take this direction."

Grabbing up his toiletry bag, he stepped into his boots and took the short path to the bathroom and its outdoor shower. The air held a crisp note, one he knew from visiting Florida in the fall would burn off as the October sun rose higher. He stripped off his sweats and stepped into the canvas stall. The pipes groaned and knocked a little, then hot water came out of the shower

64

head and poured over him. He closed his eyes and let the water pound on the back of his neck. His mind worked, going over his presentation as he soaped and shampooed.

He should have taken his brother up on his offer to review his notes as well, but he found himself wanting to do this on his own. He'd wanted to show Claire, though. To get her opinion. But she didn't seem the least bit interested in the courses or in him right now. He turned the water off with a twist.

After he toweled off he returned to the cabin and caught a glimpse of himself in the mirror set on the wall beside the bed. He fingered the gold hoop in his ear, then shrugged. He might be dressing more corporate today, but he wasn't going to get rid of the earring he'd had since his first year of college. What had started as a bit of rebellion had become his talisman. His good luck charm.

"And today I need all the luck I can get."

After he shaved he went over the presentation a few more times, then dressed in charcoal pants with a light gray shirt and dark green tie. He wouldn't wear a jacket. It would probably be pretty steamy already by eleven and he didn't need the threat of sweat marks, thanks. He took a breath, then wrapped up his papers and charts and went out to his Jeep.

The ride to the Institute wasn't a long one, but as he rolled over the trail he took a breath and let the setting seep into him. The feel of Cypress Corners itself. It gradually shifted from wild to tame to manicured as he neared the town center. Pulling to a stop in front of the Sales Center, he took a breath and let it out. The coffee shop across the street beckoned, so he went in for quick cup. And spied Claire putting the finishing touches on her drink at the service counter.

He took a few seconds to take her in. Today she wore a dark blue skirt and a shirt with puffy little short sleeves. She wore heels, and the backs of her legs were smooth and tight. From where he was standing, he could tell she didn't spend all of her time sitting behind that desk of hers. No. She got out into the recreation surrounding her. Maybe took a boat out on the lake or rode the miles and miles of bike trails all around. He cocked his head and smiled to himself. Recreation was his gig and he could show her just how to get the most out of this place where she lived and worked.

"Morning, Claire," he said.

She glanced over her shoulder and threw him a smile he didn't think she was even aware of. "Good morning, Jake."

He stepped closer as she placed the top on her coffee. Taking a sniff, he smiled. "Cinnamon?" It mixed with the vanilla scent of her and did serious things to his head.

She shrugged and lifted the cup to her lips. "I try something different in my double-shot latte every now and then." As she sipped, she growled and flicked her tongue over her upper lip. "Every day."

He smiled. "Careful there."

She shook her head. "Thanks." Her eyes ran over him, finally settling on his face. "You look very nice."

"I have a meeting at the Institute."

Her brows raised. "Oh, yes! Your presentation is this morning."

"I figured khakis and a camp shirt wasn't the way to go."

She nodded, her gaze roaming over his face. "You shaved."

Yes, he shaved. She noticed?

"Yes."

They fell silent and he took a second to run his eyes over her front as closely as he'd studied her back. "You look nice today, too."

She glanced down at her blouse, her cheeks turning pink. "I bought a couple of things."

Why was she embarrassed by that? "Come into a windfall, did you?"

The smile on her lips was a little sly and he felt a jolt of awareness.

"Hmm," he began. "Claire Callahan is keeping secrets?"

It was her turn to shrug. "Maybe."

He liked this side of her. As he opened his mouth to ask her to join him at one of the little tables her eyes flicked to the clock. Damn. His time with her was up, then.

"I have to run." She crossed to the door, then turned. "Good luck today."

"Thanks." He watched as she crossed the street and went into the Sales Center, then ordered his coffee.

Leaning back on the counter as he waited for his drink, he puzzled over Claire. She seemed self-conscious when she'd admitted buying herself something and then, when he'd asked her about it, she'd gotten a glimmer in her eye he'd never seen before. Claire with that sparkle was really hot. And just what was she hiding?

The girl at the coffee counter called his name and he grabbed his coffee and headed back outside. He'd have time to figure out Claire later. After the presentation.

Right now, he had to be on his A game.

Turning up the cobbled path to the Cypress Institute, he took in the building and its surroundings. It seemed to embody the mindset of Cypress Corners. Done in soft greens and browns, it reflected the colors of the natural landscape of the place. The edges of the building were softened with plantings exploding with colors. Blues and pinks and yellows dotted tall fringes of tan and purple grasses. His sister-in-law Harmony could most certainly name every genus and species of every flower and grass, but he could only allow that they looked very pretty. He opened one of the wide glass doors and stepped inside.

Decorated in the colors of true Florida—rich greens,

soft tans, and clear blues—it was filled with handmade rattan furniture and breathtaking photos of some of the native flora and fauna hung on the textured walls. Jake liked this space. It was comfortable and serene. He mulled that over. Those were two things he never craved but he eagerly took them in this morning.

"Mr. Chapman," the redhead behind the reception counter said with a smile. "Good morning."

He smiled. "Good morning. I'm here for my eleven o'clock."

"A little early, but Dr. Robbins will like that." She tapped on her keyboard and nodded at the screen. Facing Jake, she smiled again. "He said you're welcome to go into the conference room and set up." She pointed toward the hall to the right. "Third door down."

He thanked her and took himself and his plans toward the conference room.

"Mr. Chapman," a voice called from an open door as he passed it.

The plaque beside the doorframe declared the room to be the director's office. Jake stopped and looked at the man behind the desk.

"Good morning, Dr. Robbins," he said.

"Good morning."

The director gazed down at his desk as he shuffled at the papers scattered on it. His glasses sat on his balding head as he nodded agreement at something he read. Jake waited a beat, then cleared his throat. The other man's head shot up.

"Oh!" Dr. Robbins smiled. "Just going over a few things before our meeting. I trust you're ready to wow us?"

Jake smiled back. He couldn't help but like the director. The guy seemed absent-minded but even without Harmony's glowing endorsement of the man he would see his mind never stopped working. His skin was tan and he looked like a guy who spent time outdoors hiking and biking in addition to spending his time behind a desk.

"I'm going to knock your socks off," he said.

Dr. Robbins laughed. "Good! Harmony promised as much just yesterday."

Jake felt his face flush. "My sister-in-law might be biased but she's one of my biggest fans."

71

"I'm sure it's well-deserved. Harmony doesn't take these matters lightly. If she says your plans will only help Cypress, I'm inclined to believe her."

Jake's chest swelled a little at the man's words. Here was the family support he'd missed. First for those months away in Aspen and then stuck up at Chapman in Boston.

"Then I have a lot to live up to."

The director nodded. "Why don't you go set up and I'll join you in a few minutes."

"Thank you, Doctor."

He felt buoyed by their short interchange. In a few words the director conveyed his trust and Jake was going to prove he was worth it.

***

Claire sat at her desk as the morning wore on, touching the tip of her tongue ever so lightly on the center of her upper lip. Darn, but her lip hurt. She'd burned it again, and in front of Jake Chapman. At least she hadn't spilled any on her new blouse. She glanced down at her pretty blue top. Jake had liked what she was wearing today. She'd seen that. He'd even teased her but

72

he couldn't know she'd bought her new clothes with what she'd gotten shooting pool Wednesday night. They were earned through her skill and it was always fun to show up slightly smug guys like Mark. Hmm. Jake fit that category, too. Maybe she'd challenge him to a game or two.

"I'm going to grab takeout for lunch," Tammy said as she breezed by her doorway. "Heading out to the beach again and I want to get an early start." She stopped. "Do you want anything?"

Claire shook her head. "No, thanks. I brought something."

Tammy blew out a breath. "You always bring something. Then you eat it while you sit at your desk working. You can take your lunch break, you know."

"I know."

She didn't say more, so Tammy just shrugged and continued on. She certainly couldn't tell Tammy that she budgeted everything to the penny and couldn't swing take-out more than once in a blue moon. Claire knew how much Tammy made with her sales commissions and it was about the same as Claire. So the other woman had to know what Claire made or could hazard a good guess.

How could she explain that a big portion of her salary went to Cally's care or straight into savings? As for her pool-shooting money? That was earmarked for fun, as sad as it was that buying clothes for work could be considered fun. Once again she thought about Jake's eyes on her. She'd flushed hot then. Hotter than the darn coffee in her cup.

He had a way of tilting his head slightly to one side as his blue eyes sparkled wickedly. He had to be aware of it but it never looked practiced. Who tries so hard to hit on a woman at nine in the morning anyway? And besides, who tries so hard to hit on her ever? Mark flirted but he flirted with the servers at the End Zone just as easily. She was nothing special despite Jake's appreciative glances this morning.

As she closed one spreadsheet on her computer and opened a new one, she felt a tingle of awareness. Right between her shoulder blades. A little tickle followed by a whiff of freshness.

"Hey, Claire," Jake called from behind her.

Her heart tripped so she took a second before

spinning in her chair. He leaned into her office, a wide smile wreathing his face. His eyes were bright and his face lit with excitement.

"I take it your presentation went well," she said with a grin.

"It couldn't have gone better." He stepped inside, his hands held up in front of him. "God, what a rush. I was nervous but I forged ahead and I had them eating out of my hands."

"The director loves the outdoors, so that doesn't surprise me. But the board can be a little stuffy."

"Yeah." He laughed and settled in the small chair beside her desk. "I think I convinced even them to give the courses a try when they're complete."

She blinked. "Really? I'd come see that for sure."

He stretched out his long legs and ran his palms over his thighs. "Right? But hey, that hurdle is passed."

"That's terrific. I'm happy for you, Jake."

He loosened his tie a bit and she found herself studying his strong throat. Clearing her own, she leaned one elbow on her desk and folded her hands.

"Join me for lunch," he said.

"Oh no, I can't."

"Why not?"

She opened her mouth, but really had no reason to refuse him. His mood was high and his appeal intoxicating.

"Okay."

He rose to his feet. "Good. Let's head to the Clubhouse."

Alarm trilled through her. She couldn't go through another meal totaling his purchases as she choked down a meal she shouldn't indulge in. Something must have shown on her face, because his brow furrowed. Then he smiled.

"The tavern side, Claire. They do a hell of a burger for lunch."

Relief swamped her. "Sounds great."

She slipped her shoes on and they went out onto the sidewalk. Jake was obviously still high from his meeting. His step was light and he was still grinning.

"Claire, it was amazing. I've never had such a positive response to a presentation."

"You must have made your vision clear. How could

they resist?"

He stilled her with a hand on her elbow. His eyes were intent on her face. "Do you mean that?"

She pulled back a little. "Of course. You're very persuasive, Jake."

He laughed softly, then turned her toward the tavern. "Persuasive, huh?"

"You know you are," she said softly.

He leaned close and she experienced that pull she'd felt the night he'd taken her to dinner. His expression was serious now. Compelling.

"Can I persuade you, Claire?"

She gazed up into his eyes. He looked like he was going to kiss her. Right there outside the Clubhouse. And to her surprise she wanted him to. To feel those wide teasing lips of his on hers.

"To what?" she managed to say.

His lips tilted. "To just let go?"

Her mouth dropped open. "Jake…"

He breathed in, then straightened. "Let's go eat some meat."

She mentally shook off the spell he'd cast and let

him lead her to the tavern.

Chapter 6

To just let go. Jake's words echoed in her mind all afternoon. Their lunch together garnered some attention from some Cypress folks, and she'd tried to ignore the surprised expression on Mr. Forbes' face and the speculative one on Harmony's husband Rick's. He'd even stopped by the table and she had a lot of trouble ignoring the silent communication passing between the brothers. What was Rick thinking? What had Jake told him about the awkward end to their first date? Or worse, was Harmony going to start throwing her and Jake together? She just didn't want to think about that. Jake wasn't for her, no matter how attracted to him she was.

Right now she was looking down the business end of another weekend spent like she usually did. Saturday with Cally and Sunday sitting out on her porch or maybe, if she was adventurous, taking a book and sitting out by the lake.

"I'm off," Tammy called as she did just about every Friday afternoon. "I guess you're doing the same old same old this weekend?"

Claire nodded as she closed down the open programs

on her computer. "Nothing much, really."

Tammy crossed her arms and leaned against her doorjamb. "Yet you had lunch with Jake Chapman this afternoon."

Her cheeks heated. Yes, there were no secrets in Cypress. Luckily, the only one she kept now was her father's addiction and that he was tucked safely away in St. Cloud away from the temptation of the dog track and off-track horse betting.

"He wanted to celebrate his successful presentation."

Tammy brightened. "I heard! I can't wait to get the mock-ups for the promotional material so I can add them to my pitch." She winked. "And maybe you can convince him to spend some more time here at the Sales Center to talk up the courses to potential residents?"

Claire laughed that off. "I have no sway with Jake, Tammy."

One thin dark brow arched. "Don't you?"

Claire said nothing to that and only hoped that her fair skin didn't get more pink.

"Have a good weekend, Claire," Tammy said at last.

"You too."

As her face cooled a little, Claire focused on clearing her desk for the weekend. She didn't doubt Tammy would make good use of Jake's additions to Cypress. As for herself, she had to admit that she'd like to see him working in the Sales Center now and then. His excitement was infectious and who wouldn't want to be around that? And he sure was easy on the eyes. That handsome face, those pirate eyes. That fit body.

"Go home, Claire," Mr. Forbes said as he passed her office. "Enjoy yourself this weekend."

She managed not to jump. He couldn't have any idea she was thinking about Jake's very nice physique.

"Have a good weekend, Mr. Forbes," she said back.

It was what they often said to each other, but today she was bothered a little by it. First Tammy teasing her about doing the "same old same old" and now Mr. Forbes urging her to get out of the office in that commanding tone he always seemed to have. Taken with Jake's dare to "just let go?" Darn it, even she was bored with herself.

"Maybe I'll order a pizza from the tavern," she murmured as she shut down her computer and turned off her light. "That's…a little bit different."

Locking the door behind her, she stepped outside and headed home. After a half hour spent flipping through the TV channels and finding nothing to really catch her attention, she called in her pizza order and changed into her official weekend-at-home clothes. Her favorites, actually. Gray pajama pants with Mickey Mouse on them and a red tank top. Thick cotton socks that she sometimes used to slide across her pretty hardwood floors. She scrubbed her face of her minimal makeup and pulled her hair up into a high ponytail. She smirked at herself.

"Friday-night Claire is ready for a rollicking evening," she said.

Her doorbell rang about ten minutes later and she padded over to the front door. Through the small frosted windows set on one side of the door she could see there was a tall shadow out on her porch. Single girl living alone, she peered out the peephole. And gasped.

It was Jake. What was he doing here? She look a furtive glance in the mirror to the right of the door, still seeing plain-Jane Claire staring back. Her shoulders slumped and she pulled open the door.

He was just looking at her. Expectant. She took a few seconds to take in his appearance. He wore jeans now, with those boot/sneaker shoe things. Faded jeans that showed off his long legs. His shirt was one of those soft-looking Henley ones, buttery yellow with the top two buttons undone and the sleeves pushed up toward his elbows. He looked so yummy. She gave herself a shake and forced herself to look him in the eye.

"Jake, what are you doing here?"

He grinned and held aloft a pizza box. "Dinner is served."

"You're a stalker." She placed her hands on her hips. "And why do you have my pizza?"

"Your pizza and a bottle of wine."

She saw he held a bottle in his other hand but just shook her head. "A pizza stalker."

"What, no tip?" he asked.

She tried to hide her smile. "Why are you here?" she tried again.

He shrugged. "I was at the tavern, thinking about picking up my own take-out to bring to the tent-cabin when I heard your order come in. I thought I'd be a gentleman and bring it to your door."

"They have golf-cart kids to do that," she said, referring to the delivery staff who provide door-to-door room service to residents.

"I was there, Claire."

When he didn't say anything more, she let out a breath. If she were being honest with herself, she didn't want to eat alone. She wanted to share her pizza with yummy-looking Jake Chapman.

"Come in."

He stepped inside and she shut the door. His fresh scent struck her, followed closely by delicious pizza aroma. Her stomach growled but she didn't know quite what she was hungry for.

"What do I owe you?" she asked, forcing herself to back away from him and the pizza.

He waved a hand. "You can make it up to me."

She couldn't rouse an ounce of outrage at that statement and crossed through into the kitchen. "Okay, but you're not getting a tip."

He laughed and followed her. "On the counter all

right?"

"Sure."

He put the pizza box and wine bottle on the tall counter set between her kitchen and the living room. "Plates?"

"In the cabinet to the left of the sink." She grabbed two wine glasses and set them on the counter. "You can't keep doing this."

"What? Feeding you?"

She rolled her eyes. "You're exasperating, you know that?"

His eyes sparkled. "I've been called worse."

She snorted. "No doubt."

He opened the box and peered down at the pizza. "Olives?"

"I like olives."

"But there's no meat."

"After the burger you inhaled at lunch I would think your arteries might appreciate the reprieve."

He arched a brow and sat on one of the barstools. "You ordered extra cheese, Claire. Don't talk to me about arteries."

She sat beside him and inhaled the hot scent of garlic and the earthy tones from the olives. "Just give me a piece."

He served her and himself each a slice, then poured the wine. "So what were you up to before I crashed your Friday night?"

She gestured from her ponytail to her pajama pants. "Nothing special. Can't you tell?"

His eyes lingered on her chest and she was suddenly very aware that she wasn't wearing a bra. The tank top wasn't thin but she guessed there was no disguising her reaction when her nipples tightened. Crossing an arm in front of her breasts, she reached for her slice and brought it up to her mouth.

The pizza was a treat she didn't usually allow herself. It was gooey and spicy and the tomato sauce was just right.

Thankfully, Jake took her cue and dug into his own pizza. They ate and drank for a while.

"This wine is delicious." She held up the glass and the liquid caught the light. "Blush. Very pretty."

He nodded. "I find a blush very pretty, too."

He was staring at her face when he said it, so she accommodated him with a flush on her cheeks. She couldn't stop it if she tried.

"So what are you doing this weekend?" he asked.

She demurred for a second, then shrugged. "I have errands to run tomorrow."

"Damn, I'd hoped to get you out on the lake."

"The lake?"

"Out in a canoe. I wanted to show you a few spots where the trail takes to water."

"What about alligators? Water moccasins?"

He laughed a little. "The gators, we'll check for. As for the snakes? It's best not to think about it."

Horror must have shown on her face, because he shook his head. "I'm teasing. As long as you stay away from the edges and the tall grasses, snakes aren't too big a problem. But don't worry. The animal control guys will check for them, too. Often."

She shivered. "Still."

He chewed for a bit, then swallowed. "Just a hint of danger, Claire. It adds to the experience."

"I don't like taking chances."

"I know."

She blinked and studied him. He looked very serious right now.

"What are you talking about?"

"The other night." One brow arched. "After dinner at the Clubhouse?"

Oh, she'd known it would only be a matter of time before he brought that up.

"We'd had a wonderful meal, Jake. You're a terrific date."

"Thanks, and yes we did. But later, when we were talking and you…closed up on me. You always do that."

Anger tickled at the edges of her mind. He was right of course, but he was certainly a jerk to say it.

"What did you expect me to do, Jake? Throw myself at you after one date?"

He pulled back. "No. I didn't mean that. I meant our conversation." His eyes ran over her again, interest stamped on his features. "But if you had thrown yourself at me I would have had a lot of fun catching you."

His words that afternoon struck her again. *Just let go.* Why was that so hard for her? Why was it so difficult to admit that she wanted to let things go now and then? To skip her Saturday visit with Cally and go to the beach with Tammy? To throw herself at a hot guy who'd just dropped big bucks on dinner? Hell, to go to bed with dishes in the sink?

She knew why. It was how she was made and that realization just made her sad.

Chapter 7

Jake watched as the emotions flitted over Claire's face. She'd been pissed there for a second, but now she just looked deflated. What the hell had he said?

"More wine?" he asked, holding the bottle to her glass.

"Yes." Her answer was quick.

They ate quietly after that. As unaccustomed as he was to silence, he was grateful that he wouldn't have the opportunity to put his foot in his mouth as they finished their pizza. He had no idea what was going through her mind and he wouldn't push her. Instead, he looked around her pretty little house.

It wasn't in the same neighborhood as Rick and Harmony's house and the yards were narrower but it was still situated across the street from one of the many parks scattered throughout the development. It was a one-story with an open floor plan and soaring ceilings highlighted by dark beams across the roofline. The kitchen was very clean, with white cabinets and sparkly gray counters. The glass-front cabinets bracketing the sink showed glasses arranged by height and dishes stacked neatly. Everything was clear or white with the occasional touch of blue.

Swiveling on his stool, he took in the living room.
The couch looked nice and soft. The white fabric covered
plump cushions and pillows. Smaller blue pillows were
precisely placed near each armrest, though. Picture
perfect, with the karate-chop crease right in the center.
He was seized with the urge to mess them up, preferably
while rolling around with Claire on the wide seat
cushions.

There was the surprising accent here and there,
though. Seemingly out-of-place but interesting. The
bright orange lantern sitting off to one side of the mantel,
the Magic Eight-ball on the other. The rusty iron
bookend holding up an impressive line of cookbooks on
one kitchen counter. The messy ponytail in Claire's hair.

That was his favorite, really. That ponytail. It left a
strand of hair in front of one cheek, just shy of long
enough to tuck behind her ear. It left her neck smooth
and vulnerable, and made him want to run the tip of his
tongue over it until she shivered. He had to fix this,
though. The melancholy he saw on her face that he
suspected was his fault.

He just wasn't good at this stuff. Relationship-y stuff. Fucking he could do. He could make a woman cry as she came before finally letting himself go. He could trace every inch of a woman's body and promptly forget every damn detail in the light of morning. He knew he could do that. He could fuck and forget and move on.

He didn't want to do that with Claire, though. Maybe it was because she lived in his brother's backyard. Maybe it was because he'd spent twice as much effort trying to get to know her than he ever expended on a woman. Maybe it was because when he'd told her every damn detail of his presentation she'd been completely engaged and invested.

Or maybe it was just because she was the cutest, hottest woman he'd seen in forever. He didn't want to just fuck and he didn't want to fuck this up, whatever this was.

"What do you want me to do, Claire?" he managed to ask.

She started, then stared at him with those big blue eyes. "Nothing."

That one word said it all, though. She wanted

nothing from him. He nodded and moved to get up when she placed a hand on his forearm. Her touch sent a spark through him and he looked over at her in surprise.

"Just let go," she whispered.

And then she wrapped her arms around his neck. He caught her, turning to drop his hands to her hips and hold her between his thighs. Her body was so soft, her breasts pressing just right against his chest. Her nipples teased him through his shirt and he shuddered. He was hard in the next instant and, when she eagerly rubbed against him, he didn't think she minded. The purring sound she made told him she liked his reaction very much.

"Claire," he said, bringing his lips to her. "God, Claire."

She opened her mouth over his and he kissed her back. Hard. Her taste filled him. Garlic and tomatoes and olives from the pizza. And that vanilla he knew he'd always associate with only her. When she sucked on his tongue he groaned.

He buried his face in her neck. "You're driving me crazy."

She nodded and murmured something he didn't

catch, then let her head fall back. He couldn't resist. He licked her neck like he'd fantasized about just minutes before. He had his hands on her ass now, and she wriggled as if trying to get closer. He didn't need any other invitation. Pulling back, he put his hands on her upper arms.

"Couch," he managed to say.

She nodded and licked her lips and he swallowed. Man, her lips looked so dewy soft he almost groaned again.

Tumbling with her, they messed up the pillows as he pinned her beneath him. He had to get that sexy little top off of her. He had to see if her skin was as soft as it seemed. If her nipples were as pink as he imagined. Grabbing the hem, he pushed her shirt up and out of the way. And sucked in a breath.

Pearly smooth skin covered her breasts, which were firm and round and tipped with delicate rosy peaks. His mouth watered.

"Damn, you have pretty tits."

She giggled. Actually giggled. He decided he liked this Claire, too. This easy-going girl who seemed to want him to touch her everywhere. He closed a hand over one breast and she moaned. Ah, that was an even better sound. Pinching lightly, he teased her. Her nipple puckered tight and she gasped. He couldn't wait much longer. He had to taste her. His mouth covered her breast and he suckled. Her vanilla scent was strong here under her shirt. Hot and sweet and she tasted just as good against his tongue.

She arched and he slipped an arm beneath her. Her fingers ran through his hair, tugging and pulling whenever he did something she liked. And she liked a lot of the somethings he did. Licking. Sucking. Biting.

He was hard as a rock as he pressed against her, and her cute pajama pants had a nice stretchy waistband. Slipping a hand down the front of her, he parted her curls and found her wet.

"God," he said again.

He glanced up at her and found her staring at him, her breath coming fast. "Touch me, Jake. Please."

He stroked her softly, earning a growl from her. She squeezed her eyes shut and bit her lip.

"Deeper," she whispered.

95

He smiled down at her. "What was that, Claire?"

She muttered something and opened her legs wider to him. "Deeper," she said again.

He pushed two fingers high inside her and she cried out. "Yes!"

He stroked her, in and out as he teased her clit with his thumb. Kissing her, fondling her as she rose toward climax, was the absolute best time he'd had with a woman in a long time. Just let go? Oh, he'd get her to let go. As many times as it took. He brought his mouth to her breast again and licked the nipple.

She came in a rush, bucking against his hand as he kept up the pressure. He lifted his head to watch her come and he thought he'd never seen anything so pretty. She was wild and free and beautiful, with that pretty pink blush spreading all over her body.

"Claire," he said, dropping his head to her neck.

She was dewy there. Sweet and a little salty now. She let out a little sigh as he kissed her where her neck met her shoulder.

"Wow." She took in a deep breath, which pushed her breasts more fully against him. "I've never... Not like that anyway."

He laughed, which was amazing because he was throbbing so hard now he could hardly breathe. "So this is you letting go?"

Her eyes slowly opened and she smiled up at him. "I guess so."

He kissed her lips and lifted himself up on the hand beneath her. "I liked you telling me what to do. I found it surprising, though."

She smiled as she pushed her shirt down. "And I'm surprised you liked being told what to do."

Shifting on the couch, he tried to ease the pressure on his cock. She moved to sit up and he grunted as her knee brushed against his groin. To his shock, she reached out and cupped him.

"Claire," he said, half moan, half plea.

"You're hard, Jake."

"Yeah."

Her fingers traced over him and he hissed.

"And big," she said, popping open the top button of his fly.

He had no words for that one. She somehow eased

down the zipper without killing him, then wrapped her hand around his shaft. Her fingers were soft. Delicate. Just right. It wouldn't take much for him to come right now. Right in her hand, which he didn't think he'd done with a girl since high school.

"You're killing me," he said, letting his head fall back on the couch. He eyed her from beneath his heavy lids. "You're just killing me."

She glanced up at him, eyes sparkling, and a corner of her mouth curved a bit. He could watch her face all night. Could watch the curiosity and arousal etched on her flushed features. Her hair was a mess but she looked adorable. Her teasing fingers drew his gaze quickly from her face to where she was stroking his cock.

"You need to come, too."

He nodded. Why deny it? The woman had her hand on his pulsing dick. She knew what she was doing to him. He lifted his head and looked at her face again. Didn't she?

"Claire."

"Yes?" She brushed her thumb over the top and he shivered. "What do you need, Jake?"

He bit his lip. "Make me come," he rasped.

She smiled, then brought her mouth to his. He kissed her as she straddled his thighs, using both her hands now to drive him crazy. She went tight and fast. Slow and light. She had skills he didn't think she knew she had. He was wild now, so close to coming all over the two of them. He lifted his shirt just in time to cover her hands with one of his and come hot and wet onto his stomach.

She kissed his mouth again and sat back. After a long beat, blood returned to his brain. He eyed her, read the pleased expression on her face, and laughed.

"I take it that's my tip," he said.

She giggled again and fell against him.

Chapter 8

Claire slept in on Saturday morning. Jake had stayed after their messy mix-up on the couch. They'd talked over coffee and cookies which he ate after only remarking once about how perfect they looked. It was strange sitting there with him after losing her mind underneath him. And then stroking him to climax? She'd never done that before with a guy. The few encounters she'd had in her life were limited to friends-with-benefits in college that were relationships that barely classified as friends in the first place. She'd come a few times before. But what Jake had done with her body last night? It was amazing and left her wondering just how much fun really letting go would be.

"Never going to happen," she told herself as she got up and out of bed.

It was a sad realization, but heavy petting was as far as she would let things go with Jake Chapman. She didn't want a friends-with-benefits thing again. Not at her age. And what did that leave? Professing everlasting love over a picnic on the lake? Yeah, right.

She was going to see Cally today. To check in and

find out why he'd been so fidgety last week. Maybe they'd go to the End Zone for some wings. He always liked that, getting out of the fifty-five plus environment and shooting a few games of pool. Even with his failing sight in one eye he was still a shark.

He'd taught her everything she knew about pool. She was better at it, though. Mostly because he played with emotion and she played with math. Charm could only go so far on the felt, and she usually ended up beating him pretty well. It was a point of pride with Cally when she won, though. He never pouted or bitched about it. In fact he bragged all over the place about his daughter the pool shark, even though she never tried to hide her abilities from any opponent.

After she showered and dressed, she stepped into the kitchen and saw the wine glasses still on the counter. She'd gone to bed without cleaning the kitchen! It was a small victory but she'd take it.

She hummed to herself as she washed the glasses and put the pizza box in the recycling bin, then wiped down the counter. Glancing at the couch, she saw the pillows were still all over the place. God, she'd had such a messy happy time with Jake on those pillows. She'd known he was built, but when he'd lifted his shirt right before his climax she'd nearly swallowed her tongue. His abs were perfection, and she regretted her hasty decision to never repeat last night. No, she'd wanted to lick him all over every bump and dip in that glorious body and now she was bummed she would never allow herself the chance.

Last night she'd been wild Claire. Messy Claire. A Claire she barely recognized in the light of day. Today she was once more reliable Claire. Steady Claire. The math mind of Cypress. Ugh.

She threw the dishcloth in the sink and cursed.

***

Her father's mobile home was snug and set on one of the many roads that made their even and ordered way through the retirement community. She parked under the carport next to his Thunderbird, the last car he'd earned as a bonus for Salesman of the Year. That momentous event was ten years ago, before his gambling took so much of his time he began to phone it in at the dealership. The car was looking a little dusty but the small convertible was sleek and it had a retro sixties look Claire loved.

It was poppy orange. It was her favorite color but, despite having bought some clothes and accessories in it, she would never dare wear it with her coloring. It had more of a pink undertone than yellow, and she couldn't resist buying a few things for her house in that color for a treat now and then. Yes, the car was a beauty. It made her Prius look like sensible shoes set next to f-me pumps on a shag carpet.

The postage-stamp yard was tended by the maintenance staff, paid for from the monthly dues she had taken directly out of her account. That, and the payments on the mobile home. The lot, at least, was deeded to her. Not to Cally. He'd balked but there had been no way she'd let him put his name on another legal document of possession. Not after losing his house in Melbourne three years ago.

She climbed the two steps to the porch and rapped on the aluminum frame of the screen door. She could hear the TV inside, set to one of the golf shows that seem to be on every channel on Saturdays.

"Dad?" she called.

She heard quick steps and the door behind the screen was opened. Her father looked out at her, a big smile wreathing his face.

"Claire-bear," he said, both of his blue eyes sparkling with equal brightness. "Come in, come in!"

She smiled at the nickname she'd had for as long as she could remember. She pulled open the screen door separating them and stepped into the living room. Her eyes ran quickly over everything, taking in the rumpled newspaper on the coffee table and the dishes stacked in the sink. Setting her purse on the round kitchen table, she began to straighten up.

"So how was your week, Dad?" she asked, running the water in the sink.

"Same old, same old."

His words echoed Tammy's but her father couldn't know that.

"I thought you went to Gatorland the other day."

"We did." He waved a hand and started to fold up the newspaper. "It was fun, I guess. You know, they have this zip-line thing that lets you glide over the gators?"

She straightened. "Please tell me you didn't do that."

He laughed, throwing his head back. His close-cropped silver hair caught the light coming in the big front window. "No friggin' way were they getting me up on that thing. I might be half-blind but I'm not stupid."

Claire clicked her tongue. "You're not half-blind. Have you been taking your meds?"

"Yes, honey."

He tipped his head toward the blue plastic pill tray with the little lids on each daily compartment set on the counter. Every week she filled them up for him and she saw that he hadn't missed a dose.

She smiled. "Good."

He moved around the living area, fluffing the pillows and placing them near the armrests, and she knew he did that for her benefit. She washed the dishes and set them in the rack to dry, then wiped the few crumbs off the counter. For a guy losing his sight in one eye, he kept the place pretty tidy.

She turned and leaned back against the counter, crossing her arms. "So what would you like to do today, Dad?"

He shrugged. "I'm up for anything. You know that."

She met his bright blue gaze, feeling the charm the man had in abundance. Yes, he was up for anything. She knew he would give anything to get her to drive him out to Melbourne to the track, but that was so not happening. He didn't ask outright. In fact, he never even eluded to it more than a couple times a year since losing everything. But still, she knew the desire was there. The compulsion for another big win.

Waiting a beat, she quirked an eyebrow at him. "What would you like to do today?" she asked again.

He opened his mouth, then shook his head with a laugh. "You're calling the shots today, Claire-bear."

His wording made the decision for her. "The End Zone, Dad? Maybe shoot a few games?"

"Now that sounds good to me."

They locked up and stepped down onto the driveway.

"Why don't you drive my baby today, Claire?"

Claire looked at the Thunderbird with near lust in her heart, then gave a quick shake of her head. She held one of the keys to it on her key ring since Cally couldn't drive any more. She would just continue resisting that temptation.

"No, no. We'll take my car."

He just shook his head and climbed into the passenger side when she unlocked the doors. "Electric car. Never had to deal with the things when I was on the lot."

"Hybrid, Dad. Electric and gas."

He snorted. "Like that makes any more sense?"

Cally caught her pointed look when she sat in the driver's seat and fastened his seatbelt. He opened his window to let in the fall breeze and Claire did likewise, knowing fully what would happen as they drove down the narrow streets.

"Hey there, Cally!" a trim, gray-haired woman called from her tiny front porch.

"Hello there, Nancy," Cally called back with a wave. "Going to shoot pool with my daughter today. You should come along!"

Nancy twittered. "Maybe we'll have another shuffleboard match," she returned.

Cally laughed and winked in Claire's direction.

"Nancy's a widow. Lots of time on her hands."

"I'll bet," Claire said.

"Cally, you're looking good this morning," another lady said from where she was watering her patch of lawn.

"Back atcha, Paula," Cally said.

A few of the men they passed waved and shouted to Cally too, and Claire smiled. He was a charmer and, basically, a good man. People were always drawn to him. Her mother had been head-over-heels for him since the second she met him, as she'd told Claire time and again. And he'd been a loyal husband and loving father.

That was what made all the crap he'd put his family through all the more tragic.

***

Jake sat on the tech-wood planks next to Nick, watching the boy's little legs swing back and forth as the two of them fished off the dock. The lakeside was across the street from Rick and Harmony's house, and the setting was perfect if a little tame for his tastes. He much preferred the more primitive far lake shore.

Nick was uncharacteristically quiet this afternoon, so Jake used the time to go over what had happened at

Claire's last night.

She'd been surprising. That was for damn sure. She turned him on like no other woman had in a long time and he wondered what she was up to today.

Hanging around after their couch calisthenics had been really nice, too. She'd been more relaxed than he'd ever seen her, and he flattered himself to think the orgasm he'd given her had something to do with that. She was always wound so tight. From the first, he'd wanted to know what she would be like when she let go. Now he knew.

She was incredible. And he couldn't wait to see how she'd be after he took her everywhere he longed to.

Nick shifted on the dock beside him, drawing Jake's attention from the captivating Claire. He set all lustful thoughts about the pretty redhead aside and took a breath.

The air was crisp but this close to the neighborhoods there were too many cars passing for Jake's peace of mind. He craved solitude as much as he liked to hang with Rick and his family. That wasn't really surprising, since he traveled for Chapman alone. Yes, he'd hook up with some woman now and then at the resorts or properties but he'd never bunked with them. Never hung around after scratching their mutual itch.

"Where are you going to swim, Uncle Jake?"

Once more, Jake focused on little Nick.

"Swim?" he asked.

"Yeah. Swim. On your course."

Jake got what Nick was asking then. He pointed over to the far side, knowing by now that his nephew wouldn't want anything less than the most specific answer Jake could give. "See that clump of trees over to the left?"

"The cypress?"

Jake grinned. Of course the kid would know what kind of trees they were. His mother was a plant conservationist with a botany brain.

"Yes, the cypress," Jake answered. "Part of the trail will push through the water just over there. But there will only be a little swimming."

"Because of the bridges," Nick said with a nod.

And because of the gators, but Jake wasn't going to tell Nick that. "Yep. Rope bridges will stretch across to just about there." He pointed to the bit of sandy shore visible from their vantage point. "Then the trail will continue on the footpaths."

Nick nodded. "Can I try it when you build it?"

"I'm afraid not, buddy."

"Why not?"

"It's for grownups. Not for kids."

Nick pouted. "Why not?" he asked again.

Jake opened his mouth, then snapped it shut. Why not? Why couldn't the kids in Cypress, kids of visitors and residents, enjoy an adventure?

"You know what, Nick?"

Nick gazed up at him. "What?"

"You just gave me a terrific idea."

He stood, reaching down to offer Nick his hand.

"Where are we going Uncle Jake?"

"Well, buddy?" Jake grinned down at him as they walked down the dock toward Rick's house. "We're going to your house where I'm going to talk to your dad about the idea you just gave me."

Nick beamed up him. "I'm very smart."

Jake laughed. "You sure are, buddy. You sure are."

Chapter 9

By the time Claire settled down in front of her TV on Saturday night, her head was throbbing with a dull headache. Cally had been almost manic today, joking and laughing and being pretty much the life of the party at the End Zone. They'd shot more games of pool than she could remember them playing in a long time and, even though he'd begun to flag around three o'clock, he kept up the show for everyone's benefit. Especially hers. And every time she worked the conversation around to asking for more details about what had occupied him all week he'd evaded and danced and pretty much laughed off her concerns. It was enough to set her teeth to grinding.

She'd dropped him back at his mobile home around five, made sure he was set for the coming week with his meds then picked up some groceries on her way back to Cypress Corners. A bowl of tomato soup and a green salad was a quick, cheap dinner and now she figured she'd just curl up on the couch and relax. No more thinking about her father. Or at least, no more worrying about him. He should be safe and sound until next weekend. So she'd poured herself a glass of the wine she'd shared with Jake last night and settled down for a peaceful, if lonely, Saturday night. It wasn't even seven o'clock and she was tucked in safe and sound. Whoopee.

Picking up the remote, she thumbed through the channels and settled on some movie rerun. She took a long sip of the very excellent blush wine and all but ignored the movie, choosing instead to think about everything she and Jake had done right there on her comfy couch.

Oh, his touch on her skin. She knew how to touch herself. Sometimes, when she couldn't fall asleep the moment her head hit the pillow, she'd give herself a little something-something. But those little blips in her heart rate she'd achieve were nothing compared with the mind-blow Jake had given her.

She glanced at her cellphone, charging over on the kitchen counter, and thought about calling him. She had his contact info, of course. It was in her address book synced from her computer. Eyeing the Magic eight-ball on the mantel, she considered asking it just what she should do. She had no real reason to call him. Heck, she had no reason to think he'd be free on a Saturday night.

"Right, Claire. He's sitting in Harmony's tent-cabin just waiting for your call."

He knew plenty of other people here at Cypress. He had contacts here. Contacts through his brother and through the investors at Chapman. The director of the Institute loved him. She'd heard about how well his meeting had gone. Even with as little as she knew about the particulars of adventure excursions she could feel his enthusiasm when he spoke of it. His descriptions brought it to life and the light in his eyes when he talked about the challenges? Oh, that was easily as compelling as his beautiful face and gorgeous body.

Jake wasn't for her, though. Yes, he made her feel things she'd never felt before. Yes, he was charming and so engaging she sometimes had trouble looking straight at him. Time and again she'd proven to herself she wasn't a fling type of girl. And Jake Chapman wasn't a relationship type of guy. Not that she was looking for one. With her father to care for and herself to take care of? She had a full plate, thanks.

Her doorbell rang and she jumped. Her mind flashed back to the surprise of finding the man himself on her doorstep last night. Despite living in the lightning capital of the world, she knew that lightning wouldn't strike twice. Not for her.

Unfolding from the couch, she set her wineglass on the coffee table and stood. It was weird that someone was stopping by but, then again, it was only seven o'clock on a Saturday night. Not everyone in Cypress was holed up in their houses with only wine for company.

The frosted glass beside her door showed her a now-familiar silhouette and her heart did a silly flip. What the heck was Jake doing here?

She checked her appearance in the mirror as she had last night, relieved that she still wore some makeup and had on a bra tonight at least. Taking a breath, she pulled open the door.

Jake stood there in jeans and a blue polo shirt, holding a bag of obviously-Chinese take-out given by the red dragon printed on the plastic outer bag. She could smell the garlic and grease and took another deep breath.

"Hello, Jake."

He grinned at her, his eyes bright. "I have to talk to you."

She blinked. "Me? Why?"

He opened his mouth, that lovely mouth, and then just shook his head. "Let me in and I'll tell you."

"I think as the spider I'm supposed to say that to the fly."

He laughed and stepped inside. "Then I'm the fly bearing Chinese food, Miss Spider."

As she closed the door he walked into her kitchen like he lived there and set the bag on the counter. "Have you eaten?"

"Soup and salad." She closed the door and joined him. "But if you have an eggroll in there I wouldn't say no."

He reached in the bag and pulled out a wax paper sleeve. "An eggroll."

Smiling, she got down two plates and a couple of forks, then settled on the barstool next to him. "You're going to spoil me."

He arched a brow. "With an eggroll? You're a cheap date."

She snorted and he covered his eyes with a groan.

"Damn, I didn't mean that the way it sounded."

She waved a hand. "Never mind. Now, why did you have to talk to me?"

He dumped some fried rice on his plate and took an eggroll for himself. "I was out fishing on the dock with Nick today and the kid asked me a question. Hell, the kid asked me a dozen questions, but that's him. The Riddler."

Claire smiled at the image of Jake and his nephew out on the dock as Nick peppered him with questions.

"Yeah, I've been the target a few times," she said.

Jake nodded and scooped up some of his rice. "So he asked me if kids could use the adventure trails and when I told him no he asked why not?"

"And you said…"

"I said, why not right back at him."

"I don't understand."

"A kids' course, Claire. A place like the adults' courses, scaled down and a hell of a lot safer."

Claire sat back, her hands in her lap. "That's a great idea! Have you talked to Rick?"

"Yep." He took a big bite of his eggroll, chewed and swallowed. "He loved the idea, of course. It was his son's, after all."

"The development would love to have an attraction like that."

"A kids' zone will be the perfect place for children to wait for their parents to complete their courses or, heck, even their rounds of golf," Jake said.

"No, not just that," she said. "Do you know what places like fun zones and safari rides make from locals and tourists?"

He smiled at her. "No, but I bet you do."

She nodded vigorously. "Tons, Jake. And the Cypress kids go off property for those tame trills. Why not get them right here?"

"And also draw people down from Orlando and in from the coast as well."

"Yes." Claire's mind worked. "Cypress could sell annual passes for Florida residents, like all the attractions do. As well as day passes, of course."

"Damn, that would be perfect."

"It would boost business for everyone on property."

"Tell me I can use that when I present this addition?"

Proud that she could help him, she nodded. "Sure."

She rested her elbows on the counter and leaned toward him. "Show me what you're thinking it will look like."

Jake beamed at her, then grabbed the folded menu from the bag and flipped it over to the nearly-blank side. He bit his lip as he took a pen from the cup beside the napkin holder and sketched out the addition to his adventure trails. Claire watched his lovely mouth and couldn't help but want to bite him herself.

"It will mirror the large courses," he said. "Scaled down and made to meet safety requirements for little guys."

He held the pen in his strong fingers and she forced her attention to the sketch instead of what she knew he could do with those fingers.

"That's preliminary anyway." He turned on his stool and looked at her, his brows raised. "Well?"

She traced a finger over the winding trail he'd drawn, then held her hand flat over the paper. "Jake, it will be fantastic."

His eyes flicked downward and for a second she thought he was embarrassed by the compliment.

"Thanks."

119

"But why did you have to talk to me about this?"

He met her gaze then. "You're smart, Claire. You know the ins and outs of Cypress."

Her heart sank a little. "Yeah, I'm the money mind."

He smiled. "Maybe, but that's not all you are."

She tried to ignore the fluttering in her belly. "What else am I, then?"

He leaned a little bit closer and she could smell his fresh scent. "You're the girl I want to kiss."

She swallowed. "Jake, I don't think this will work."

He tilted his head to one side, that pirate hoop glinting in the lights from the pendants hanging over her counter. "What? Friends can't kiss?"

Claire bit her lip to hold in her smile. "Friends?"

His lips slanted upward in one corner and she licked her own.

"What would you call what we are?" he asked.

She opened her mouth, but couldn't put it quite into words. Maybe she would give him a little bit of truth. "Jake, you're here for a limited time and I'm just a convenience."

He frowned. "Like hell."

His vehemence startled her. "Then you tell me what we are."

"Claire, look. I might only be here for a short time but I sure as hell don't think you're just convenient. And yeah, I think we're friends."

The truth slammed into her. "Fuck buddies," she said softly.

"No. Friends." Heat filled his blue eyes and he gave a slow shake of his head. "Besides, that's not quite true."

No. She had to give him that. They hadn't slept together. But even she had to admit it was only a matter of time. He was just too damn tempting and she was just too damn lonely.

"So why are you here?" she asked again. "Tonight?"

He leaned closer still, his face close to hers now. "I like you, Claire. I'm not just after that brilliant mind of yours."

Her entire body was humming now and he hadn't even touched her yet. "Then what are you after?"

He laughed, low and soft. "These pretty lips." He brushed a feather-light kiss on her mouth as his hands stroked up her thighs to settle on her hips. "And this gorgeous body."

Her heart tripped again and this time she didn't hesitate when his mouth settled on hers for a real kiss.

He held her close as she opened her mouth, both of them groaning as his tongue slipped inside. He tasted like eggroll and spice and she was hungry for everything he could give her. He didn't wait for them to get to the couch. No, he pulled her shirt up and over her head and her bra was a thin lace barrier to nothing. She couldn't be embarrassed. Not with his hands stroking over her. Not with his fingers pinching her nipples in that fantastic way they had last night.

"Jake," she whispered.

"Yes," he said, bending his head to kiss her throat.

"Don't stop."

He stilled, then gave her that low laugh again. "I don't plan to."

She reached for him, under his shirt to stroke that perfect torso. He trembled beneath her fingers and one glance at his crotch told her he was as turned on as she was.

"Couch," she murmured.

He nodded and stood, and she took the opportunity to push his shirt higher. Lifting his arms, he let her take it off him, showing his chest and abs to perfection. The light smattering of dark hair over the ridges and valleys made her palms tickle as she rubbed her hands over him.

"Very nice," she said.

"Thanks."

His voice sounded shaky and that little chink in his confidence did a lot for her own. He drew her closer, bringing that lovely chest up against her breasts. His body felt hot and hard and her nipples tightened through the lace cups.

They kissed again as they made their way to the couch. She pushed him down but before he could tug her down on top of him she fell to her knees.

"I wanted to do this last night," she said, stroking over him. She nipped him through his jeans with her teeth. "I want to put my mouth on you now."

"Christ, Claire." His head fell back. "Just your hands nearly killed me last night. But your mouth? Damn."

Lowering the zipper, she soon held him in her hands. Again. Then she licked him and he moaned long and low.

Her fingers trailed over his fit belly as she began to stroke and suck him.

He tasted fresh here, too. He was huge and hot and she let herself indulge in every ridge and dip as she took as much of him as she could. He groaned and stroked her hair as she did her best to drive him out of his mind. She would never forget this guy. Just maybe she could give him something he'd never forget. At least for a little while.

"I'm not going to come on my belly again tonight," he rasped, arching ever so slightly toward her as she moved her mouth over him. "I want to come inside you."

She lifted her head then, willing her pulse to slow enough so she could make sense of what he was saying. "I don't think that's a good idea, Jake."

He gazed down at her, his eyes like blue fire. "Why not?"

"I…" *I don't do flings. I know you're just here because it feels good.* None of those things would make sense to a man like Jake.

"I don't know," she finally said.

He breathed in, his chest expanding in a way that set

124

her pulse racing again as he considered her lame answer. Then he shrugged a shoulder. "Okay, Claire. Another time, then."

And there it was. Dismissal wrapped in a promise. She knew all about promises. She never counted on promises.

She bent her head and gave him what he needed until he shouted his release to her beamed ceilings.

Chapter 10

Jake tried to think as his body hummed with the aftermath of what Claire had just done to him. Christ, he'd thought she'd blown his mind last night!

"Christ, Claire," he managed to say, opening his eyes a bit.

She sat on the coffee table, her body still leaning toward him as she watched him with her blue eyes bright. Her breasts were nearly visible to him through that surprising pink lacy bra and, damn, if she didn't look adorable and very proud of herself.

He sat up and tucked himself back into his jeans. "What you did to me."

She shrugged and her cheeks flushed pink.

"You know, turnabout is fair play," he told her.

Her mouth fell open and he felt himself getting hard again.

"I don't think—" she began.

He held up a hand to cut her off. "You don't think that's a good idea."

She shook her head, her eyes sad now. What was she thinking in that incredible mind of hers? She was clearly talking herself out of whatever naughty thoughts she'd been thinking while she was going to town on him. He wouldn't give her the chance to send him away. Not until he drove her as crazy as she'd just driven him.

"Come on, Claire." He took her hands in his and tugged. "Tell me you're not all tingly just thinking about my tongue on your skin."

She didn't say anything to that but her breath quickened, making those gorgeous breasts rise and fall. His mouth watered for a taste of her creamy skin. Of those rosy pink nipples.

He grasped her arms and pulled her closer. "I want a taste of you. Another sweet taste."

"Jake, I don't think—"

He groaned. "Just stop thinking, Claire." He pinned her beneath him on the couch. "For the next few minutes just feel."

She seemed to give up her inner struggle in a big way. Wrapping her arms around his neck, she kissed him. "Taste me, Jake." Her tongue ran all over his neck. His chest. "Taste me."

He eased her jeans off and her little scrap of

underwear, as pink as her bra, felt silky beneath his fingers. He'd stroked her last night. He'd made her come and now he was going to lick her. He could hardly wait.

Pushing her bra cups aside, he pushed up her breasts and suckled one of her nipples.

"So sweet," he groaned. "Sweet Claire."

As he lightly bit down, she squirmed beneath him, eager for what she knew he was going to do next. He tickled her navel with the tip of his tongue before nipping her through her thin panties. She gasped and arched sharply, and he knew this was going to be quite a ride. She smelled sweet here, too. Delicious.

Putting his hands on her round little ass, he lifted her again and removed her panties. "Spread your legs."

She did, her thighs parting wide. She was pretty and pink here, to no surprise. Rosy and ready.

"Strawberries and cream," he murmured, stroking the soft red curls hiding her clit.

"Please, Jake."

He dragged his eyes from her pretty flesh and threw her a smile. "Yes, friend?"

She half-laughed half-groaned and tilted herself

toward him. "Don't make me beg. Again."

He kissed her mouth, then fell on her. Every stroke brought her closer. He could feel her tightening. Swelling against his tongue as he gave her everything she allowed tonight.

"Come, Claire," he said, licking her as his fingers stroked inside. "Come."

She thrashed on the couch, covering her breasts with her hands as she began to tremble. "Oh, God…"

He kept up the pressure, bringing her higher and higher until she bucked and moaned. He held her as she came, gentling his touch as she gasped his name.

She was a little out of it as he lifted his head from her delicious body. Bringing his face to hers, he nuzzled her cheek, her ear.

"Isn't that better?" he asked.

She took a deep breath and opened one eye. "You don't have many woman friends, do you?"

He grinned. "Nope. You're the first."

"No surprise there."

He lifted himself so she could shift to sit beside him. "And why is that?"

She shook her head and readjusted her bra. "Because no woman could be around you after that without giving you whatever you wanted."

"And friends don't, um, indulge each other?"

"Not if they want to stay friends. Believe me, I've had a couple 'friends with benefits' relationships and let's just say those guys aren't my friends any longer."

He wanted to strangle any guy who'd been in the precise position he was in right now. That jealousy was as foreign to him as the whole friends-with-benefits concept.

"We're not 'friends with benefits,' Claire." He stroked her cheek and it was as soft as the rest of her. "I've never had that either, by the way. We're friends."

"Friends." Her lips pursed and it was like the light went out of her eyes. "For now."

He doubted he could say anything to convince her he genuinely liked her. Not with her still gazing at him like he'd just given her the moon. Not with her taste still on his tongue.

So instead he kissed her until she was pliant and soft and cuddly there on her comfy couch.

***

Even on Monday morning Jake was still thinking
about Saturday night at Claire's. Yes, he thought about
the sex. Or the almost-sex. She was incredible and turned
him nearly inside out. When they finally slept together,
and they were going to sleep together, it would be
phenomenal. But the conversation before and after what
he thought of as the climaxes on the couch? That had his
head taking on its own obstacle course this morning.

He hadn't lied. She was his first woman friend. Why
the hell was that, anyway?

He liked women. The ones in his past were fun and
good times and easy. He'd take them to dinner and then
they'd take him downtown. If they seemed to want more
than what he wanted to give, none of them had ever said
a word to him. In fact, he had little contact with them
after scratching their mutual itches. With Claire though,
he'd wanted to stay. Like Friday night. Just stay and talk.
Weird.

He did like her, though. He liked hanging out with
her. Liked talking to her. Liked getting her gifted opinion
on his ideas. She was grounded and real and he did count

her as a friend. No, he'd never had a woman friend before. Not even fuck buddies, really. Just one- or two-night stands.

He couldn't figure this out now, though. Not when he had to approach the developer about the additions to his plans. He'd emailed him and Forbes had agreed to meet him for coffee this morning. So now he was at the Sales Center, leaning to one side as he peered down the hall toward Claire's office.

"Good morning, Jake," Tammy said as she breezed down the hallway, nearly bumping into him.

He stepped back and ran his eyes over her. With her neat little suit showing lots of leg, her smooth curtain of black hair and her perfectly applied makeup she looked put together and hot, but she wasn't what floated his boat lately. No. Lately he seemed to prefer a cute little redhead with a pencil tucked behind her curling hair who bit the lipstick off her lips as she worked. One who screamed when she came and made him want to do the same.

"Good morning, Tammy. I'm just waiting for Mr. Forbes."

She tilted her head to one side. "He's meeting you, isn't he?"

"Yes."

"Then why are you here?"

Why was he there? To try and catch a glimpse of Claire, maybe.

"I thought we'd walk over together," he said in lame answer.

Tammy stared at him and he managed to keep his expression even. He was saved from embarrassment when Forbes stepped out of his office.

"Jake, my boy! Let's go see what they're brewing this morning."

Jake nodded and pulled himself from the hallway. Claire's door was open as usual but now he'd have to think of some other excuse to see her this morning.

"Now, what is it you wanted to talk to me about?" Forbes asked as they walked across the street to the coffee shop.

"I have an idea for an addition to the courses," Jake said, holding open the door for the developer.

"An addition?"

133

Jake nodded as they stepped up to the counter together. "I ran it past Claire and she seems to think it would bring a lot of business into Cypress."

"Claire?" Forbes ordered his coffee and stepped back. "When did you discuss this with her?"

Saturday night before she sucked me off. Jake mentally shook his head and smiled. "The other night when we, um, bumped into each other."

Forbes furrowed his brow. "If Claire thinks its financially sound I can believe it."

Jake ordered his coffee and they stood together at the end of the counter to wait. "I'm eager to get the okay from you before I go ahead and sketch out plans."

The girl behind the counter called the developer's name and then Jake's. Taking their drinks, they headed over to a table set near the window.

Forbes took the lid off his coffee and took a sip. "Now, what is this addition and how can it make all of us more money?"

Jake chuckled. "It's a kids' course, Mr. Forbes. A safe and age-appropriate course for children."

The other man's eyes sparkled. "Residents and

visitors would eat that up."

"That's what Claire said." Jake drank from his own coffee, then set it aside. "We'd be able to draw traffic from the coast and up in Orlando, too."

"Damn, that would be incredible. I like it."

"So I can draw up something to show to the Institute?"

"Sure, sure. What does Chapman think about this?"

Jake bit his tongue before saying he wasn't going to risk running this past his father. Bill Chapman wasn't exactly a risk-taker and Jake didn't want him putting the kibosh on his plans.

"I was going to wait until I had some numbers crunched."

"You should borrow Claire for that, Jake. She's a marvel."

Yeah, she was. "I wouldn't want to put more work on her plate."

"I'll ask her for you." Forbes grinned. "The girl loves it when I challenge her."

Jake didn't doubt that. She took any chance to prove her worth to Cypress. Why she thought she had to, he couldn't guess. It was clear she was valued here.

"If Claire has the time free, I'd love to meet with her," he told Forbes.

Forbes took another sip and nodded. "Good. Let me talk to her and then the two of you can make arrangements to get together."

"Thanks." Jake thought for a minute. "It will be nice working with a friend on this."

His meaning was lost on Forbes but Jake's mind was already filled with just how much time he could possibly make this task take.

And just how much he was going to enjoy working with his sweet friend Claire.

Chapter 11

Claire threw her empty yogurt container in the trash and stood. As she crossed to the fridge in the break room, Rick Chapman stepped inside the room.

"Hi, Rick," she said, grabbing a bottle of water from the fridge door. "Want a water?"

"Sure." Rick took the offered bottle and leaned against the doorjamb. "Sorry you couldn't make it for dinner last night."

"Yeah. I was busy."

It was a lame excuse but the same she'd given Harmony when she'd called with the invitation yesterday afternoon. She'd known Jake would be there and after what they'd done Saturday night? How the heck would she face him without thinking of his handsome face between her legs? Oh, the things he'd done to her with that tongue. Those fingers.

"So, what's up?" Rick asked.

Her cheeks heated but she managed to shrug a shoulder. "Nothing much." She grabbed a bottle for herself and closed the fridge. "Just getting everything ready to enter the end of month numbers when they come in."

Rick nodded and tapped a finger on the side of his bottle. "Then you're not going to talk about getting together with my brother?"

Claire sucked in a breath. "What?"

Rick smiled. "Forbes told me all about it."

"Mr. Forbes?"

She stopped breathing as the room began to slowly spin. This couldn't be happening. Her boss couldn't know about her doing his latest favorite son on her couch! Oh God, no. What would he think of her? Would he ever trust her with the Cypress accounts again if he knew she couldn't keep her hands to herself? Forget about her reputation. Her life might be swiftly and completely shot to hell.

"Yeah, Mr. Forbes." Rick's brow furrowed. "What has you all ruffled? I thought Jake talked to you about his kids' addition to the adventure courses."

Her breathing resumed and she shook her head to steady it. "Yes. But I didn't know Mr. Forbes… What's this about Mr. Forbes?"

Rick straightened away from the jamb. "Are you

okay, Claire? You don't look so good."

"I'm fine, Rick." She leaned against the fridge and tried to look cool and collected. "Just fine."

Rick studied her for a long minute, then shrugged again. "Anyway, he said you and Jake were going to get together and crunch the numbers regarding the potential of the addition."

That made sense. Her boss was always enlisting her help on side projects like this. "It's the first I'm hearing about it, but I'm sure Mr. Forbes will let me know."

Rick nodded. "No moss grows underneath that guy's feet."

Rick was right there. The developer was always moving forward on something or other. He was the driving force behind Cypress Corners and his energy was contagious.

"I guess I'll be working with Jake, then," she said.

"Don't look so thrilled, Claire." Rick laughed. "My brother doesn't bite."

"No." Claire swallowed thickly. *He licks and sucks and kisses.*

"All right. See you later. Harmony has been making

noise about having you over to dinner soon, since you turned her down last night."

"I'd love that. Really."

"Good. Have a good one."

And with that Jake's brother took himself and his innocent questions out of the break room and Claire sank back down at the table.

"Claire?" Mr. Forbes called from down the hall.

She stood and crossed to the now-empty doorway. "In here."

Her boss soon appeared, a big smile wreathing his face. "Claire, I'm afraid I have some extra work for you."

She nodded. "Rick just told me. Something about working the numbers on the additions to Jake's project?"

"Yes. See? I told Jake you love it when I give you these special assignments. That you love a challenge."

"I'd be happy to help."

"So get with him and arrange a meeting. Those numbers could be useful for the Institute and Chapman Financial."

Useful for Claire's job and for Jake's, apparently. There was no way she was going to get out of this.

"I'll do that."

"Great." Mr. Forbes turned to leave, then turned back to her. "Jake told me he'd enjoy working with a friend on this."

Her smile was frozen in place until her boss left her alone again. Jake had told her boss that they were friends? She didn't know what kind of game Jake was playing but she was up for it. If he wanted everyone at Cypress to think they were friends, who was she to deny it?

"Working with a friend, huh?" She chuckled to herself. "We'll see how he likes staying the friend zone the next time we're together."

She didn't know if she could keep her hands off of him but if he wanted to play it this way, so be it.

***

"So what have you and Claire been up to?"

Harmony's innocent question sent a shiver up Jake's spine. He feigned intense interest in the fat plastic bricks he and Nick were using to build a tower on the living room floor as a movie about flying dragons played on the big screen.

"What are you talking about?" he asked.

"Rick said the two of you were going to be working together?"

"Oh." His shoulders relaxed. "That."

Damn it. He knew his mistake the second the words left his mouth.

"Hmm." Harmony wiped down the counter, then settled her folded arms on the granite. "That's an interesting reaction."

"What do you mean?"

"You obviously thought I was talking about something else. Something other than your project."

"Nope. Just the project."

Harmony laughed softly. "Yeah, right."

Jake risked a glance at his sister-in-law. "What do you know?"

Her eyes lit up and she grinned. "Aha! Then there is something to know!"

Jake groaned. "Drop it, Harmony. Please?"

She slowly nodded. "On one condition, brother. Promise me you won't hurt her."

Jake stood, running his hands over his thighs.

"We're friends, Claire and me."

She shot her gaze to Nick, then back to him. "Friends…?" Her words trailed off as her brows rose.

He knew she meant the dreaded "friends with benefits" crap. "Nope. Not that kind."

Harmony's lips pursed. "Good. As much as I want to see Claire happy—"

"You know I'm not the guy for her," he cut in. "I get it."

It was what he expected and the reputation he'd done nothing to deny for too many years to count. She must have seen something on his face though, because her gaze turned tender.

"I know you don't mean to hurt anyone but you have to admit you're not exactly a steady Eddie."

"No, I'm not. And I never pretend to be."

"Yeah, that's what Rick said."

Jake blinked. "Wait. You two talk about me? About my relationships?"

She put her hands on her hips. "Do you ever *have* any relationships, Jake?"

"No," he said honestly. "Why are we talking about

this, anyway? Claire and I are friends."

"That's all?"

He wouldn't tell Harmony that the memories of Claire and what they'd shared had filled his thoughts over the past few days. That he hoped to get naked with her soon. That was too much information for his brother's wife to have and Jake wasn't a kiss-and-tell kind of guy.

"I like spending time with her. She's a great girl."

"She's my best friend in Cypress, Jake. The best friend I've had in a long time."

"Is this some kind of a warning?"

She shook her head. "No. It's a statement of fact. She's my friend and if you say she's yours I'll believe you."

"Good."

"But make no mistake. I'm not the powder puff I appear to be."

Jake smiled. "So my brother has told me."

"If we have an understanding then we'll drop this." She looked over at Nick again. "For now."

God, he was starting to hate those two words. Claire

used them to keep him at a distance and Harmony used them to issue warnings.

Rick came home and that seemed to finally put a cork in Harmony's interrogation. Jake took the opportunity for escape his brother's arrival afforded.

"I'm gonna get going."

"Why don't you stay for dinner?" Harmony asked.

"Thanks, but I think I'll just grab some takeout from the Clubhouse."

Rick eyed him and Jake wondered what else he and his wife had talked about. "You sure?"

Jake nodded. He crossed over to Nick and gave him a kiss on the top of his head. "Be good, little man."

The little boy flicked his eyes from the screen for a split second before turning back to his dragon movie. "Bye, Uncle Jake."

Jake slapped his brother on the shoulder and kissed Harmony on the cheek.

"I hope I didn't run you off," she said softly.

"Not at all."

"What's this about?" Rick asked.

"Friends, bro." Jake winked. "Just friends."

145

He drove to the Clubhouse and went into the tavern to order a burger and some fries. Settling at the bar, he asked the bartender for an autumn ale on draft and waited for his dinner.

The conversation with Harmony wasn't what he'd expected tonight. She had it right, though. He wasn't boyfriend material for anybody. His brother knew it. Claire knew it. It was what it was and he wasn't going to try to change now.

His phone rang and he glanced at the screen. "Damn it." He answered with a sigh. "Hi, Dad."

"What's been going on down there?"

Bill Chapman's bluster was just what he needed right now.

"Working on the project."

"You met with the Institute."

"You know I did."

"You get with the developer?"

"Yeah. I'm working on an addition to the plan actually. Adding a kids' course to bring in more guests."

"And more revenue," Bill said. "Good plan."

The praise was given flatly so Jake accepted it in like

tone. "Thanks."

"How's your brother? And Nick?"

Jake thought he heard a little desperation in his father's voice and could guess the reason.

"They're both good. Nick is growing up fast."

"Yeah. I see that on Facebook. Kid's a looker. All Chapman."

Jake made a sound of agreement. He wondered if Rick knew their father trolled his site for any information about him and his son. It was a little creepy and he made a mental note to let Rick know.

"I should have the numbers ready to present in a week or so," Jake told him.

"You working with that pretty little redhead?"

"Yes."

Bill grew quiet and Jake didn't like the sound of that. Usually he laughed about Jake playing the field and scoring big.

"Let me know when you have something concrete, Jake."

Jake knew a dismissal when he heard it. He'd heard enough from the old man over the years to recognize when Bill Chapman's mind was on to other topics.

"Bye, Dad."

Bill ended the call and Jake sipped his ale. He and his father had no better a relationship than the man had with any of his children. Rick had found happiness away from Chapman Financial and Jake was just biding his time until he could do the same. It was the reason he took assignments far and away from Boston.

He thought about Cassie and wondered what their little sister was up to. She was wilder than Jake but in a totally different direction. Where he was all about building things she was about taking them down. And apparently having a blast with her euro-trash friends as she did so.

God, they were all so fucked up and all because of Bill Chapman. His desertion of their mother so long ago. Her unending devotion to him up until her death despite the lack of any attention apart of throwing money at the kids he had nothing to do with. Maybe Rick had it right. Maybe it was time to leave the old man for good and make his own way.

What sucked was that Jake had been playing at life

for so damn long he had no idea how to make a real future for himself.

His meal came in a tidy little bag and he paid. Getting back in his Jeep, he thought about heading over to Claire's. No. She didn't deserve a booty call. He hadn't even bought her dinner this time.

He took the rough path to the tent-cabin and put thoughts of his screwed-up family and his screwed-up life out of his head.

Chapter 12

By Wednesday afternoon Claire was on pins and needles. She knew the call was going to come. That she was going to have to put her money where her mouth was and meet with Jake to work on his project. Seriously work as the money mind of Cypress.

Every time she heard the soft chime sound, indicating the front door opened, she jerked in her chair. She admitted that she found herself looking for him around corners. At the coffee shop. In the lobby. But he'd been scarce and she felt his absence, as silly as that should be. He had a life, though she didn't know what that entailed.

He'd had dinner at Rick and Harmony's last night. Harmony had told her that when she and Nick had stopped in to say hello to Rick. Her friend had looked at her like she was searching for something. Had Rick told her how weird she'd been the other day when he'd innocently asked her about Jake? That would be just terrific.

"Are you up to anything tonight?" Tammy asked, poking her head into the office.

Claire swiveled in her chair as she shook her head. "Nope. Why?"

"I'm having a lingerie party at my townhouse." She winked. "Toys, too."

"Toys?"

Tammy raised her perfectly-plucked brows. "Toys, Claire. You know. A girl's best friend?"

Claire's cheeks flamed. "Oh, toys."

"Yeah. You're welcome to come."

Claire opened her mouth to refuse when the door chime dinged. "Thanks, but I don't think so."

Tammy waved a hand. "Come on. I bet you could use a friend."

"She already has one," Jake said from the hallway.

Tammy yelped and stepped back. "Jake!"

Claire just stared at him. He was wearing a soft-looking Henley shirt and jeans that did something really nice to his perfect body. His hair was brushed back but still a little unruly, like he'd just raked his long fingers through it.

"Right, Claire?" he asked, his eyes sparkling. "You have a friend right here."

151

Claire groaned.

"Um, that's not exactly what we were talking about," Tammy said.

Jake's brow furrowed. "Oh? Then what?"

Claire jumped to her feet. "Thanks for the invite, Tammy. Another time, maybe."

Tammy looked utterly confused but she nodded. "Okay." She dragged out the word. "I'll drop off a catalog before I leave."

Claire nodded until she was gone and then covered her face with her hands. "God."

"What's wrong?" Jake shut her door, trapping her in the office with his big body and his delicious smell. "You're all red. Usually you only blush when I'm making you crazy."

She lowered her hands. "Yeah well, you're making me crazy right now. Tammy just invited me to a lingerie and toy party."

He stared at her for a beat, then laughed.

"What's so funny?" she asked.

"Then I was right."

"About?"

"The friend Tammy was talking about? That was a little something-something to make you…blush."

"Yes, it was."

He nodded. "And I was right on another count, too. You already have one of those."

She leveled a gaze at him. "You, right?"

He splayed a hand over his chest. "Yes indeed."

She shook her head. "Look, friend. If we're going to be working together that other stuff has to stop."

He leaned close and tapped her nose with his finger. "What other stuff would that be?"

She turned away. "You're not going to make me say it," she whispered.

He chuckled this time. "All right. I'll stop teasing."

Risking a glance at him, man he looked good, she braced herself and forged ahead.

"What time do you want to get together?" she asked.

He shrugged, then settled in her swivel chair. "What's good for you?"

"I'm free tonight."

His smile widened. "Me, too. Want to do dinner first?"

She bit her lip, then noticed his eyes riveted to her mouth. "Um, sure."

He leaned back, causing his shirt to lift and show the tiniest bit of his abdomen. "Want me to bring pizza again?"

"No, because we'll just end up on the couch again."

The words came before she could stop them, but there it was.

"And?"

"Friends, Jake." She put her hands on the armrests and leaned close to him. "We're friends. The other stuff is over."

"Why?"

"Why?" She straightened. "Why? Because we're working together now."

"On one project. And only a piece of one project, really."

"Still, that's the truth of it."

He stared up at her, his eyes a compelling shade of blue gray now. "If that's the way you want it, I'll be good."

She knew what he was doing. He'd be good, all

right. He'd be good all over her couch like last time. She had to get on surer footing and fast.

"How about we shoot some pool?" she asked.

Jake blinked and she knew she'd caught him off guard. "Shoot pool? Where?"

"The End Zone. Have you been there?"

"The sports bar? Sure. Once or twice with my brother."

"We'll eat there and shoot a couple of games. I always think better after playing."

He nodded and stood, a smile playing over his mouth. "Claire, you're full of surprises."

She grinned at him. "Just wait until tonight."

***

He was going to lose his mind. There was no other outcome from this night. He was going to lose his fucking mind.

Jake deliberately pulled at his bottle of ale, watching as Claire set up another shot. She'd changed before he'd picked her up. Casual Claire was a sight to behold.

Her jeans hugged her round little ass and dipped just low enough that he glimpsed a sliver of her panties in the back. Purple tonight. He narrowed his eyes as they traveled over her back to her smooth neck revealed by her ponytail. Was she wearing a matching bra?

The crack of the ball drew his attention back to the game he was rapidly losing. Without doing a damn thing. She'd broken the racked balls and hadn't given up a shot to him yet. Solid ball after solid ball sank precisely where she said it would and he was left standing there like a doofus. Leaning on his pool cue and hoping his half-hard dick wasn't visible in the lights hanging over the pool tables.

"Eight ball right side," she said, reaching over to smack the winning shot into the pocket. "Ha!"

She straightened and turned to him, her eyes bright and her smile wide. Jake felt it like a punch to the gut.

"Damn, Claire. I never took you for a shark."

"Not a shark, Jake. Everyone I play with knows what I'm capable of."

He eyed the other guys in the place. More than one of them had watched Claire as she'd whipped his ass, and it wasn't because they had any money riding on the outcome. Nope. It was because she looked so damn hot when she was playing.

"I'm glad we didn't play for money," he said, taking the rack from her to set up the next game.

He started to rack the balls as she chalked her cue. "I think the stakes are a little bit higher than the usual twenty bucks."

"Oh?" He stopped and caught her eye. "Just what are we playing for, then?"

She blinked those big blue eyes at him, trying to look innocent but he could see the gleam there. "Maybe the stakes are to be named at a future date?"

His blood pounded low and he nearly growled at her. "And maybe the winner can name them?"

She laughed, a free sound that sent her head tilting back. His eyes ran over the curve of her throat, then followed the natural course down to the deep V of her plain yet sexy yellow t-shirt.

"What's so funny?" he asked, stepping closer.

She met his gaze. "I don't intend to lose, Jake. So don't go making any plans to spend your winnings."

Jake wanted to kiss her right then. He wanted to bend her over the pool table and run his tongue all over her until she begged him to take what he wanted no matter who won the game.

"Can I get in on the action?" a guy asked, stepping up to the table.

Claire smiled at the newcomer, a good-looking country boy type. "Hey, Mark."

The guy gave Jake the once over and Jake did likewise. "Mark, is it?"

Mark nodded and stuck out his hand. "Yeah. I'm a friend of Claire's."

Jake shook his hand. "Jake Chapman." He shot a look at Claire, whose cheeks had gone that shade of pink he so liked. "I'm a friend of hers, too."

Mark tilted his head toward the table. "So what are the stakes? You know, our girl rarely loses. I'd watch what I bet if I were you."

You're sure as hell not me and cool it on the "our girl" stuff. Jake managed a smile. "Don't you worry about me."

"Hidden talents?" Claire asked, leaning one hip against the table.

Jake and Mark both faced her.

158

"Just because you haven't seen them yet doesn't mean they're hidden," Jake said. "I get to break this time."

"Can I play?"

"Nope." Jake smiled at Mark. "No offense Mark, but this is between Claire and me."

Mark stared at him, then a light dawned in his eyes. Good. The sooner the guy realized Claire was Jake's if she was anybody's, the better.

"Okay, then." Mark walked over to Claire. "I think you have a real challenger here. Maybe you'd better watch out."

"Oh no, Mark." Claire slid a glance in Jake's direction. "What we have her is just a friendly rivalry, isn't that right, Jake?"

Jake made a show of giving her an easy shrug. "Whatever you say, friend."

She laughed again, this time softer and from the throat. Jake nearly groaned but at least whatever was zinging between them was clear enough to send Mark away to find his own game three tables away.

"I can't wait to see your moves," Claire said, waving

a hand over the racked balls.

He held his stick steady and leaned down. "Haven't you seen a few of them already?"

She gasped and he smiled to himself as he broke. The balls scattered but didn't rest until the purple and white spun across the felt to sink in the left side pocket.

Eyeing Claire, he sized up his shot. He'd sunk the twelve ball so now the stripes were his.

"Fourteen corner pocket," he called, hitting the ball and sinking it as he'd planned.

He heard Claire grumble something but kept it up. The thirteen and ten followed, and he couldn't resist taking a peek at his opponent. Her eyes were trained on the table, her head doing that tilt thing he now knew meant she was calculating. If he missed a shot, he was screwed. He knew it. She knew it. Hell, even Mark probably knew it.

He didn't miss, thank God. He sank all the stripes and all that was left on the table was her solids and the eight ball.

"Eight ball, right." He cracked the cue ball against the eight and it went down like a stone.

"Damn it," she whispered.

It was his turn to lean on his cue, all casual. "I believe we're even."

She took a draw from her pumpkin ale and shook her head. He realized she hadn't taken a sip the entire time he was shooting, no doubt too anxious to take her eyes off the table.

"So best two out of three?" she asked, reaching in to grab some of the balls out of the pockets.

He grabbed the others then stepped closer, just to watch the color creep up from her cleavage to her cheeks. "Stakes?"

She stared him dead in the eye. "Oh, no. When I'm the winner, I'll name them."

"When?" he countered with a raise of a brow.

"Yes, when. You got lucky."

She began to rack the balls and he leaned close to her ear. "I haven't gotten lucky yet, but I'm going to."

Clicking her tongue, she shook her head. "Getting cocky, Jake. That could lead to your downfall."

"I don't doubt that, believe me."

She grinned, then focused on clearing the table

before he even got in a shot. And focus she did. Time and again she'd step back from the table and tilt her head, using that fantastic brain of hers to size up her shots. And time and again she sank the damn ball she'd called until she was the one facing him over the felt with triumph in her eyes.

"Shit," he muttered.

"That about sums it up."

Chapter 13

They put their cues in the rack, signaling the table was free. Claire grabbed her purse as the two of them walked back into the bar. She looked absolutely adorable with her head held high and her little nose in the air. Smug looked good on her, though he hadn't taken her for the smug type.

"So what are the stakes, Claire?" Jake had to know.

"I'm still thinking."

"Now I'm scared."

She grinned again. "You should be. Why don't we get to work and worry about the stakes another time?"

"Here?"

She shrugged and waved to the girl working behind the bar. "This is as good a place as any. We've determined that working at my place isn't an option."

"Ah, the couch."

She dipped her head. "Yes, the couch. And forget about your place by the lake."

"What do you know about my place by the lake?"

"It was Harmony's, remember? She told me when you moved out there."

163

"Yeah. All by my lonesome."

"I'll just bet."

She slid into a booth and he sat across from her.

"What do you mean?" he asked.

"It's a beautiful spot, Jake. Very romantic."

"If you say so."

"Pristine waters. Spanish moss hugging everything. Outdoor shower."

He leaned over the table. "Have you been fantasizing about my shower, Claire?"

She pulled back, but he didn't miss the telltale flush. "No! I just thought you'd have company out there once in a while."

"I haven't had any company out there."

She looked relieved and he wanted to ask why. But he supposed that would overstep the ridiculous friendship rule.

"It does get lonely out there," he said, leaning back to stretch out a bit. "Want to come keep me company? Maybe take a shower?"

Her eyes ran slowly over him, making his soft knit shirt feel a little too tight. He was grateful the table was hiding his groin right now.

"If my couch is dangerous I don't want to think about your shower."

He shook his head and just stared at her until she took out her tablet and brought up her notes. He'd play it her way. Stay in the friend zone without any extracurricular activities. She was thinking about him out there by the lake, though. Thinking about him in that shower. He was sure as hell going to think about her there now. And he was going to have to do something about it he hadn't had to do in years.

They'd eaten before shooting pool but he ordered some potato skins anyway. As they ate he went over the plans again, illustrating the age groups and number of kids who could participate at a given time. The load the course could accommodate and how long each progression should take. Putting it to her that way helped her calculate returns based on a few different price structures and she suggested an annual pass which would be a great addition. The course would kick ass. There was no question.

Before long, the financial wizard inside her took

over and he was bowled over by her attention to detail as she worked with the numbers he'd given her. She wore such focus on her face he was as turned on by that as he was by the sweet scent clinging to her.

"There's no question the addition would prove profitable," she said in conclusion, sitting back and raising her head. "Anyone can see that."

"Because you made it crystal clear."

She beamed at him and he felt that familiar jolt again.

"Thanks."

"You're good, Claire. Really good."

She tucked everything back in her bag and slid out of the booth. "That's why they pay me the big bucks."

He knew she was only half kidding. Her salary had to be pretty good but from what he'd seen she didn't live like it was. Her clothes were nice but not obviously pricey like Tammy's. Her house was modest and that dinky electric car was super economical. Maybe she was saving for a rainy day. She was obviously a planner. Something he had no experience with himself.

He stood and waved her ahead of him toward the

front doors. "Now, back to our bet."

She shook her head at him. "I haven't decided on my prize."

He didn't hide his open appreciation of her face and form. "I can think of a really good one."

"N-nope." Her voice was a little shaky and he knew she was turned on. "Not going to happen."

He held the door open and she got into the Jeep. "We'll see." He walked around and got behind the wheel. "Now, where to?"

"Home."

"Home?"

"Yes. I'll email you all the worksheets, Jake. Then you can present them to Mr. Forbes and the Institute."

"You should come with me."

"Oh, no." She waved her hand. "That's not my thing."

"Come on. You've never been in on the presentations? Not even in the Sales Center?"

"That's Tammy's gig. So not me."

"That's a shame, then. You should see your face when you're talking numbers."

She stared ahead, her shoulders slumped. "Yeah, that's me. Math geek."

Was that really how she saw herself? Amazing.

"No. You look hot when you get all focused, Claire. It's something to see because it's beautiful."

Her head shot up and she pinned him with her gaze. "Really? Beautiful?"

"Oh, yeah." He started the Jeep and put it in gear. "It's a shame we're stuck in the friend zone."

He let that statement hang in the air between them until she was forced to answer.

"Why?" she asked.

"Because if you turn me on focusing that attention on your numbers you drive me out of my mind when you're focusing that attention on me."

The temperature inside the Jeep climbed but neither of them said anything until he pulled to a stop in front of her house fifteen minutes later.

"Um, good night," Claire said.

Jake turned his head to look at her, then gripped the steering wheel to keep from grabbing her to him. "Good night."

She let herself out and he watched as she climbed the front steps and disappeared into her house. He breathed in deep, slow and steady, until his body stopped throbbing enough so he could focus on driving back to the tent-cabin.

He hadn't lied. Everything about her turned him on. Her face. Her body. Her mind. He was in trouble with this girl. Trouble he'd never been in before.

He cursed and pulled away from the curb. He had to get himself in control or he would lose what was building between the two of them.

Even if he didn't know what the hell it was.

***

Claire stepped out onto the veranda wrapping around the Sales Center. It was Friday afternoon and the weather was at last holding a touch of autumn. Beyond the Clubhouse she could see the leaves on the trees lining the golf course were just starting to turn a little. The real show wouldn't be until sometime in December, but fall was coming. There was no doubt about it. It was enough to make her crave one of those pumpkin lattes the coffee shop started serving this week. She'd saved a little bit on

169

meals this week, what with Jake picking up the tab at the End Zone. The heck with it. Her day was waning and she wanted a pumpkin latte.

"Hello there, Claire!"

She looked up as she crossed the street, seeing Lettie waving her over. Smiling, Claire approached her. Lettie, or Charlotte Fairfax, was a staple in the town center. She currently sat at what Claire knew was her favorite table beneath the purple crepe myrtle.

"Hi, Lettie. What's up?"

Lettie shook her head, her silver bangs brushing over her brow. The woman wore a large straw hat, a flower-print smock, denim overalls, and a pair of bright green Crocs. She was outrageous and sweet, and knew every bit of gossip that could be found in Cypress. She was in her seventies but looked closer to fifty. She claimed this was due to healthy living, big hats and the liberal application of sunscreen.

"Now, don't you just want to know?" Lettie countered.

Claire blinked. She knew the woman had the goods about any romantic entanglements in Cypress, and that she prided herself on her accuracy. She claimed to have hit the nail on the head regarding Harmony and Rick's love and stated time and again that she was eager to ferret out another great love story. Since Claire didn't consider herself a viable candidate for love stories great or small, she felt completely safe. There was no way Lettie would want to poke her little upturned nose into Claire's decidedly dull business.

"I take it you've heard something?" Claire asked.

"Heard? No." Lettie smiled coyly. "Seen? Oh, yes."

Claire looked up and down the main street, then turned back to Lettie. "What did you see?"

"That delicious Jake Chapman, Claire. He jogged past here just about ten minutes ago."

Claire fought to keep herself from looking down the street again. "Oh?"

"Yes. My, that boy is fine."

"Lettie!"

Lettie raised her brows. "What? A woman of a certain age can't find a strong chest and tight butt attractive?"

Claire laughed. "All right. I'll give in on that one."

"Are you, what do the kids say, hitting that?"

Claire's mouth dropped open. "I... I am not."

Lettie clicked her tongue. "That's a shame. Now, my late Mr. Fairfax could burn up the sheets but I bet that boy would make a fair show of it."

Claire thought of how he'd set her on fire, twice, on her couch. His lips. His hands. His body.

"Yeah," she murmured.

Catching herself, she shook off the image and faced Lettie. The woman was smirking as she lifted her glass of sweet tea.

"Seems to me I'm not the only one thinking about him in less than honorable terms."

"We're friends," Claire rushed out.

"Friends?" Lettie sipped her tea, then placed her glass back on the table. "Seems to me your friendship could burn pretty hot if you fanned those flames I see in your cheeks."

Claire covered her cheeks, then dropped her hands. "Well. I was just going to grab a latte before heading back to my office."

"Don't let me keep you." Lettie's eyes sparkled but

she didn't say anything more about Jake or heat or anything else.

"I'll see you, Lettie," Claire said as she turned to go into the coffee shop.

Oh, the woman was good. She could see straight through to Claire's dirty little mind about Jake. After she got her pumpkin latte, she stepped back out onto the walk. And nearly ran right smack into him.

"Hey!"

She stepped back and ran her eyes over him. God, he looked good. He wore a sleeveless t-shirt over loose running shorts but the clothes clung to his sweaty body. His hair was half standing up, half plastered to his head, and his eyes were bright.

"Hi, Jake," she choked out.

He grinned as he rested his hands on his knees and bent over. "I was just finishing up my run." Straightening, he lifted his shirt and wiped his face with it. "It's finally starting to cool off a little in the afternoons."

She nodded, her tongue thick in her mouth. His abdomen and chest were visible as he wiped and, even

173

after the shirt dropped back in place, she couldn't get the delectable image out of her head.

"What are you up to?" he asked.

Holding her cup aloft, she shrugged. "Pumpkin latte."

"Ah, another harbinger of fall."

"Yeah." Jeez, she sounded lame.

"I'm going to be meeting with the Institute on Monday. It would be great if you came along."

"I don't think so."

He looked disappointed, but it couldn't be because she wasn't going to be there. He just wanted another ally. A friend. That was all.

"Okay." He watched her for a long minute, then touched her shoulder. "I'm going to finish with a few laps in the pool."

Oh, now that was an image she didn't think she wanted to get out of her head.

"Enjoy."

He turned and ran toward the swim club, his long legs eating up the sidewalk until he disappeared around the corner. Taking a deep breath, she closed her eyes and counted to ten.

"Friends, huh?"

Lettie's voice reached Claire and her eyes popped open. The woman was grinning ear to ear.

"Friends," Claire said back to her.

Crossing back over to the Sales Center, she wondered if she should rethink this whole "friend" thing. Seeing Jake all sweaty had her thinking things that were definitely not friendly at all.

Chapter 14

About a week later, Jake was up at the Sales Center
going over the final preparations before ordering
materials for the start of the construction. The Chapman
investors had come through, even on the addition of the
kids' course. It was just a matter of getting the best price
quotes and having the land cleared.

He was using a vacant office off the hallway, and
imagined he could almost smell Claire's scent when she
came in. He'd beaten her here, which was a feat in itself.
When he hadn't seen her Prius in the parking lot he'd felt
a little smug himself. He didn't want to think about what
kept her on a Friday morning. He was just pleased he'd
get to see her. As friends, of course.

When she came in, he knew. Her steady steps. Her
soft humming he didn't even think she was aware of. It
was the sound she made when she took the first sip of her
latte. It was the same sound she made when he licked her
right behind her ear.

"Good morning, Claire," Mr. Forbes called from
down the hall.

Her soft yet firm greeting in return set Jake's pulse

tripping. Damn. He'd been trying it her way. Keeping things friendly even after seeing her all hot and bothered the other day out on the walk. She'd practically drooled on him there in front of the coffee shop. When she turned her focus solely on him, it was a definite turn on.

Pulling up the bids he'd gotten, he thumbed through the possibilities. He'd try to focus himself on the job at hand. Then he could join the guys when building the thing commenced.

Grabbing up the phone, he called the best offer for grading and prep and accepted their offer. Taking a page from Claire's book, he'd actually set up a spreadsheet of names, dates and prices to track his progress. He smiled. Wouldn't his father shit his pants when he saw Jake was not only getting the job done but documenting it for the investors?

That task accomplished, he brought up the sites where he'd placed orders for the apparatus needed to augment the rough scape. They were still in process, but that was all right. It wasn't even November yet, so his January first test runs shouldn't be delayed.

"How's it going, Jake?" Tammy asked from the

open doorway.

He glanced up and saw her leaning a bit to show off her cleavage. She had pretty nice cleavage, if her skin was a little too tan for the recent change in his tastes. Nope. He preferred a pale creamy tone since getting a certain redheaded CPA naked.

"Great, Tammy. Have you made progress with the brochures?"

She nodded. "Yes! I have some formatting to go over but I wanted to run the content and photos by you."

"Sure. Any time."

Her smile was quick. "How about tonight?"

He met her gaze and saw the blatant interest there. If he wanted to he could have her tonight. That was clear. It had been clear on his last visit to Cypress and, apparently, she was still open to whatever he wanted. Pity he didn't want it.

"I'm going to be busy tonight," he told her.

"Oh?"

She wouldn't leave it alone. He knew it and she knew he knew it.

"Going over to Rick and Harmony's. We have to

make our Halloween costumes for Saturday night."

"Ooh, I love Halloween. I can't decide if I want to be a sexy cat or a sexy nurse."

"I don't doubt you'd rock either one."

She grinned. "Are you up to trick-or-treating after Nick gets put to bed?"

There was that offer again. He shook his head.

"I'm sure I'll be pretty beat. The kid runs me ragged."

She nodded. "Okay. Rain check?"

"Sure."

"I'll email you the brochure mock-ups, then."

"Thanks."

She left and he was relieved the tail end of their conversation had been back on the topic of business. He didn't need her thinking anything more was possible. Not when he was tangled up with Claire and this friendship thing. He had to get out of that zone and fast. Before he went crazy trying to keep his dick in line with his head.

***

Claire finished her latte and turned from her desk to stare out the window. Her view wasn't anything spectacular but she still liked looking out at the tall trees and lush landscape. The town center was very picturesque too. Though less than fifteen years old it had the look and feel of an historic downtown in New England. It was nothing like the art deco pinks and yellows she'd grown up with in Melbourne but she found it was beginning to feel a lot like home.

"Jake's working down the hall," Tammy said behind her.

Claire took a breath, then turned in her chair. "Oh?"

"Working on the adventure courses. Construction should start by next week."

"I know."

"You know?"

Claire bit her lip. "Yes. Jake told me that was the plan. Last week. He told me last week."

Tammy nodded. "When the two of you were going over the numbers." She leaned against the doorjamb, her brow slightly furrowed. "Is there anything between you two, Claire? I know you've gone out a couple of times."

"Yes. We've had dinner."

"And?"

Claire couldn't lie but she didn't want the truth to get out. The fact of what she'd done with Jake before wising up.

"We had a good time. We're friends."

"Just friends?"

It was so much like her conversation with Lettie last week that she nearly growled with frustration. "We're friends," she said again.

"I just asked him out and he turned me down flat."

That shouldn't have given Claire a little flutter in her belly but it did. "Maybe he's busy."

"That's what he said but I got the impression there was someone else."

Claire held herself still. "You did?"

"He seems interested in somebody, Claire. Somebody he's been palling around with lately maybe?"

"I don't know what you're asking me, Tammy."

"Look." Tammy stepped inside and leaned toward her. "If I'm off base tell me, but I think there's something between you two."

Claire stared at her. "Something?"

"He's hot. Smoking hot, actually. I would be all over

that if he gave me any encouragement. But I don't want to come between whatever is happening between you two."

"Nothing is happening." *Not anymore.* "Nothing at all."

"Whatever could happen then. You're friends, right?"

"Yes."

Tammy shrugged. "Friendship has been known to turn into something else. I've never had that happen but I don't generally have any guy friends. Not without benefits, anyway."

Claire nodded. "Well, we're staying friends."

"Whatever you say. But I won't try to come between you two anyway. I anticipate messiness and I'm so not about the drama."

"Okay."

Tammy smiled and sailed back out into the hall. Claire sat back and went over their strange conversation in her head. It boiled down to two things. Tammy had asked Jake out and now she wasn't going to come between him and Claire.

There was something between them, of course. As far as she was concerned, she couldn't stop thinking about him. Not while she'd been out with Cally on Saturday. Not while she'd gone running for the first time in weeks on Sunday morning and not while she'd eaten a lonely dinner Sunday night. Not while she'd fantasized about him in that shower just like he'd said she would. It was driving her crazy but it couldn't be any other way.

She'd tried to put him out of her mind. She'd baked a ton of cookies and even brought in a plate that morning to set in the break room. Mr. Forbes had raved about them and she'd been secretly pleased that he recognized she could do more than balance the books.

"Hey, Claire."

She jumped at the sound of Jake's voice. "Hi!" she answered a little too brightly.

He leaned in, a half-smile on his face. "What are you up to tonight?"

"Why?"

"I'm going over to my brother's for dinner and to work on Halloween stuff. Would you like to come along? Maybe bring some more of those pumpkin spice

183

cookies?"

"The iced ones?"

He nodded. "Yeah. I only got one before Mr. Forbes devoured them."

She bit her lip. "I certainly baked enough of them."

She caught what she'd said and waved a hand. "I had a lot of brown sugar on hand so I just doubled the recipe."

"Great." He turned to leave, then faced her again. "It'll be fun."

"Yeah. It'll be fun."

He left and she turned back to her desk. Placing her head in her hands, she groaned. How was she going to keep him in the friend zone when he was even tastier looking than her iced pumpkin cookies?

***

Saturday she didn't have to take Cally out of the retirement community for their day together. The rec center in his community had a Halloween party for the residents and he was thrilled to show off his daughter to all his friends. She'd had a good time, too. It was fun watching him in his element. He'd charmed the ladies

and kidded the men. Everyone seemed to love Joseph
Callahan. That was for sure.

He seemed better to her today, too. Less frantic and
more at ease as they talked about the week he'd just
passed. It was pleasant and normal but she still couldn't
shake the feeling that she was waiting for the other shoe
to drop.

Now she was spilling bag after bag of mini candy
bars into the big bowl she reserved for Halloween trick-
or-treaters. Thursday night dinner at Rick and Harmony's
had been fun. Easygoing and fun, just like Jake had
promised. There had been heat, of course. Zinging
between them whenever their eyes met. He'd teased her,
too. Offered her a place on the couch next to him just to
get a rise out of her. She'd been very good, though.
Toeing the line and keeping things on the up and up
between them. Even when Jake tried on bits and pieces
of the pirate costume he'd decided on, she'd fought the
battle and won. She'd given him all the looks and sounds
of benign encouragement. She'd been the friend
encouraging him and that was all.

Her body wanted to tell her mind to shut up and go

with it. Jake's eyes had sparkled like his earring as he'd tried to gauge her reaction to his posturing and it had been pretty hard to keep from jumping him right there in front of his family and innocent nephew!

Harmony had watched them closely, though. With that same glint in her eye Tammy had the other day. Was it that obvious Claire had the hots for Jake? He was a gorgeous guy. What woman wouldn't want to jump him if given the opportunity? Claire Callahan, that's what woman. She was keeping herself from indulging for the stupid reason that she didn't want to get hurt. Maybe getting a little bit hurt in the long run would be worth it if she had a little bit of fun in the short.

"You can figure this out, Claire. Make the numbers work. How many times can you have Jake before your heart gets involved?"

That was one math problem she couldn't solve. Too many variables. There was one constant, though. Jake wasn't looking for long-term. That should free her to indulge herself in the short-term. Her heart was the only one she'd be risking. She didn't take risks, though. She liked things steady and dependable and…boring. Maybe it was time to take the tiniest risk if it could yield her a big fat reward. And what better reward was there than Jake make-her-scream Chapman?

By the time the first trick-or-treater rang her doorbell, she was very pleased with herself. She'd made her decision. She was done with the friend zone and ready to play with the big boys. Unwrapping a mini Snickers, she popped it in her mouth and chewed.

If she played her tricks right, she would get her own treat tonight.

Chapter 15

Jake was amazed at how exhausting trick-or-treating with a three-year-old was. Harmony and Rick were the real troopers, carrying the little guy's haul as they trekked from one house to the next. Jake reached into the bag Rick was holding and snagged a Mars bar.

"Really, Uncle Jake?" Rick teased. "Nice."

"Hey, just trying to save the boy's teeth. That's all."

Harmony laughed. "Just because you're dressed like a pirate doesn't mean you get to maraud and pillage."

"No marauding, I promise. Pillaging? That's another thing entirely."

She rolled her eyes, making her look almost silly in her fairy costume. Rick was rocking his Captain America suit, a perfect counterpoint to Nick's tiny Thor persona complete with blond wig. Jake's pirate knee breeches were a little tight, but the ends of the wide cloth tie around his waist hung down in front of his groin. His puffy shirt was open at the neck and the red bandana around his head went perfectly with his earring. He wore hiking boots instead of pirate ones, because there was no way in Hell he was going to tromp around Cypress in heels. Not even for all the candy in Nick's bag. Together the four of them looked as silly as any of the other groups making their noisy way up and down the streets of Cypress.

They were almost to Claire's street. He wanted to ask for a special treat from his girl tonight. His friend, he mentally corrected. She was his friend.

He'd been unable to keep from teasing her the other night. She was just so damn cute when she was flustered. He'd known from the first that it would be a lot of fun to ruffle her a little. He'd ruffled her a lot since that first meeting and the girl didn't disappoint.

"Whose house is this?" Nick asked, as he had at every house they'd visited. His little plastic pumpkin pail swung with every step.

"Claire's," Harmony answered.

"Oh, good! She's a good baker. Do you think she baked candy?"

"You don't bake candy, but I bet she has some great treats," Rick said, sliding a look at Jake.

Jake smirked at him. Rick hadn't said as much but his brother was sharp. He'd seen something between Jake

189

and Claire before and the other night seemed to clinch it. Rick knew Jake wanted Claire. There was no use denying it to his brother. Should the subject come up in a way other than subliminal? Jake would just assure him that he would never do anything to hurt their friend. At least that promise he could make.

Nick ran up the steps and rang Claire's bell. She opened the door with a smile, her lips wobbling a little when she saw who it was. Then that smile came back a whole lot brighter. Bright enough to knock Jake off his boots.

"Trick or treat!" Nick yelled.

Claire pretended to consider her options. "Um, treat."

She dug into the bowl of candy, grabbed a big handful for Nick, then dropped it into his pumpkin.

"Boy!" Nick looked into his pail. "You do have great treats, Claire!"

"Uncle Jake certainly thinks so," Rick said.

Jake shot his brother a look over Nick's head, then risked a glance at Claire. Whoa. She wasn't putting on the friend act at the moment. No. She was looking at him in probably the same way he was looking at her.

"Hey, Claire," he managed to say.

"Hey, captain."

He grinned and closed one eye. "Arrrgh."

She laughed, that easy laugh he could never get enough of. "Shiver me timbers."

He opened his eyes wide and ran them over her. She wore jeans again. And another soft-looking t-shirt under a cute blue cardigan that matched her eyes. Her hair was loose and flowed over her shoulders. Oh, he'd like to shiver her timbers all right. All night long.

"How's the trick-or-treating been going, Nick?" Claire asked.

"Great, Claire. I got tons and tons of candy."

"Which we'll freeze and dole out in manageable portions," Harmony said.

"Oh, you're no fun," Rick teased. "First Grandma drops off that tofu-cocoa nib thing and now you're rationing the candy?"

Harmony swatted him on the arm. "My mother's tiramisu is delicious. Admit it."

"I admit nothing."

Jake laughed. "It's not like anything Claire makes but it was pretty good."

"We're all partial to Claire's baking," Harmony said.

Claire seemed to take their banter in stride but her eyes never totally lost that heat he'd glimpsed. He was so coming back here later. To find out just what was going on in that gifted mind of hers.

Another group tromped up the steps behind them and Jake turned to Nick.

"We better get a move on, Nick. Treats wait for no man."

"Okay," Nick said.

The little boy looked longingly into Claire's bowl again and she gave him a few more pieces.

"Make sure and eat those before your mom freezes them all, Thor," she said.

Harmony laughed and they all turned away from the doorway. Jake could feel Claire watching his tight breeches as he walked away. This was very interesting.

Maybe it was time to do a little marauding after all.

***

Claire hadn't even bothered hiding how much she

liked looking at Jake the pirate tonight. Why would she? If she wanted to take a little bit of a risk she had to put herself out there. So she'd let him see how hot she thought he was. It was no hardship. Those ridiculous tight pants hid nothing. And that open shirt? She wanted to tear it off of him with her teeth. Even the little hoop in his ear looked naughty tonight. Like the rest of him. Naughty and delicious and all hers if she wanted. Because his eyes had sparked and lit in answer to her come-on.

"Shiver me timbers indeed," she laughed to herself.

Just after eight o'clock her bowl was empty and the street outside nearly so. Flicking off her porch light, she signaled she was closed for business. Not for Jake. No. If he rang her bell she'd ring his right back.

She looked through her meager wine collection set in the rack on her counter. No sign of blush but there was a nice white she'd had for some time. Needing something to do, she took down two glasses and hoped she wasn't drinking from both of them before her night was over.

She poured the wine into one of the glasses. As she took her first sip, there was a soft knock at her door. Her pulse raced and she set the glass back down and smoothed her damp palms over the front of her jeans.

"Relax, Claire," she told herself. "You don't even know who it is."

With the porch light off, there was no silhouette to give her visitor's identity away. Resorting to the peephole, she peered out and could just see her pirate standing there. The streetlight behind him lit his long, lean edges. Legs braced apart. Stance expectant. God, her body heated with a rush that took her breath. Bracing her hand against the door, she waited a beat. Then she pulled open the door.

"Captain," she said.

He grinned at her. "Trick or treat."

"Treat, Jake." She stepped back and waved him in. "Treat."

He came in and waited until she closed the door and then he stalked toward her. She held herself rigid, her every muscle threatening to give out at once.

He swept the bandana off his head and brought his face to hers. "Are you sure about that, friend?"

She groaned in mock protest, then nodded. "Oh,

yeah."

He grabbed her now, holding her tight as he kissed her. Hard. He tasted so good, like the candy bars he'd eaten and that freshness that was Jake.

His open mouth ran over her cheek. Her throat. "I've wanted to kiss you again, Claire." He nipped the cord of her neck. "I've wanted to get you under me since that night at the End Zone."

His words made her blush and heat and she wrapped her arms around his neck. "I wanted to be under you, Jake. God, I wanted to be under you."

He pulled back and stared at her, his breath rasping over her. "Then, why?"

She could pretend to not know what he was asking. That he didn't want to know how screwed up she was that she kept him at arms' length for no good reason. No good reason at the moment, that was.

"You're all about living in the moment, Jake." She ran her fingers over the sexy stubble on his cheeks. "I'm not good at that."

He peeled her sweater off her shoulders, stroking her skin with his thumbs as he did so. "You're great at that.

Trust me."

She began to shake her head but he cupped the back of her head and brought her in for another kiss. Opening her mouth, she took him in. Her body sparked everywhere she touched him. Her breasts. Her belly. Her thighs. He felt so good pressed tight against her.

Reaching into his puffy shirt, she stroked his strong chest. He felt so warm. So solid. She lifted her lips a hairsbreadth from his. "Here's to the moment, then."

He groaned softly and nipped at her lips. "In your bedroom, Claire."

A tremor of excitement went through her. "M-my bedroom?"

He grabbed her butt and pulled her up against the ridge of his erection. Through the thin material of his costume pants, there was no mistaking how much he wanted this. How much he wanted her. It was heady and sexy and she couldn't imagine sending him back to the friend zone at the moment.

"My bedroom," she said with determination.

"Yeah, your bedroom." He ground against her, then turned her around and placed his hands on her shoulders.

"No climaxes on the couch tonight."

His words, whispered in her ear, made her laugh and melt at the same time.

She grabbed his hand from one shoulder and tugged him down the short hallway to the master bedroom. It wasn't a long trip. Her house wasn't big.

"God, these jeans." He cupped her butt cheeks and squeezed. "I wanted to peel them off you when we were shooting pool, Claire."

She couldn't help wriggling against him, up so tight against her butt. "And then what?"

"And then?" He growled and turned her to face him again. "I wanted to do what I'm going to do now."

She saw the desire on his face. His expression was almost feral. Tearing his pirate shirt open, she licked his chest. She breathed in his scent and her mouth watered.

He shrugged out of it and held her head, then brought her face up to his again.

"Do it, Jake." She flicked her tongue over his lips. "Do what you wanted to do now."

In a flash she was on her bed, her shirt off and her jeans dragged down her legs. He toed off his boots and cursed as he fought with the buttons on his knee breeches but then he was nearly naked. Gray boxer briefs hugged his impressive length.

Leaning up on her elbows, she eyed him hungrily. "You're beautiful."

He slowly shook his head. "Nothing compared to you, Claire. That focus? Those eyes? I wasn't kidding. You make me so damn hot."

She felt Jake's focus all over her skin as he crawled onto the bed. They tangled on the comforter as they shed their underwear and Jake began to kiss her. Everywhere.

Like the last time, he caressed and licked her breasts, using his teeth and tongue to draw her nipples tight. His fingers were deep inside her, stroking and teasing as she arched into everything he was doing.

"I'm tasting you again, Claire." He gave her tingling breasts each a kiss, then moved down her body. "You're delicious, you know that? I can't wait for another taste."

He was between her thighs now, spread wide because she couldn't get enough of him. Almost in her next breath, she was coming all over and crying out his name.

Dragging his body up over hers, he brought his face to hers again. "Ah, Claire."

She opened her eyes and peeped at him. He was waiting. She knew it. He knew it. He was waiting to get the okay from her to continue down this rocky path. There were obstacles. In her mind, at the very least. But at this moment, with echoes of pleasure still trickling through her body, she would happily skip down that path naked and singing. Living in the moment had its definite advantages.

"I hope you have a condom," she whispered.

His eyes widened, and then he gave a vigorous nod. "Oh, yeah. Two of them."

***

Jake tortured himself a little bit more before easing off her pliant body. Finally, he climbed off the bed to dig in his right boot. Those pirate pants he'd worn didn't have pockets. And after seeing the invitation in Claire's eyes earlier he'd snagged a couple of condoms from Rick's bathroom when he'd gone back to their house.

Turning back toward the bed he took in the beauty of Claire spread and ready on her bed. Her breasts rose and fell rapidly and her eyes were slightly out of focus. All that strawberries and cream skin was flushed and rosy and he wasn't going to waste another second before getting inside of her.

After taking a few spare moments to open the wrapper and take care of things, he kissed her again and then he was there. Right where he needed to be. She fit him perfectly.

They moved together, her every sound of pleasure reaching deep inside him as his own climax soon threatened. Bracing himself on his arms, he closed his eyes and held on to his slipping control. This girl took everything from him and he nearly lost it himself when she came.

"That's it," he said, burying his face in the crook of her neck. "God, I love making you come."

Her skin was dewy and slick and he flicked his tongue over her throat. Sweet and hot.

"Jake!"

He knew she was climbing again. When she trembled beneath him, when she squeezed tight around him, he thrust three more times before they both went over the edge together.

Falling on her, he held on tight as he slammed his eyes shut. His head spun as his blood pounded in his ears. She'd pleased him before, with her hands and her mouth, but this? He felt like he'd lost consciousness there for a couple of seconds.

"That was…" she sighed.

She didn't finish her sentence and he was damned if he could. He just withdrew and hug her closer. She'd wrung him out and he'd never felt so good.

He had no idea what came next but he had a few more weeks in Cypress. And the more time he could spend in Claire's bed, the better.

Chapter 16

Claire had woken to an unfamiliar feeling Sunday morning. It wasn't a bad one. Nope, not at all. It was the sensation of having a guy curled up against her in bed. She'd turned slightly, and found Jake's eyes open as he regarded her with that sexy half-smile. And when his earring glinted in the light slanting in through her blinds she thought she'd never seen anything hotter. Or more dangerous.

She'd expected him to leave after the time in her bed, after the two times, actually. To her surprise he'd stayed the night. But in the morning with that easygoing smile? He'd been just too much to handle. So she'd made some sort of excuse and he'd taken her cue to leave her alone.

Now it was Monday and as she carried her pumpkin latte to the office she tried her best to assure that no one in would guess what she'd shared with Jake Saturday night.

Tammy walked up to her as she neared the doors to the Sales Center. "Hey, Claire. Happy Monday."

Claire smiled. "How was your weekend?"

"Okay." She held the door open for Claire, then walked through. "I was happy to get out of Cypress, though."

"Why?"

Tammy quirked an eyebrow. "You weren't here last year, Claire. Halloween can be downright scary."

"Ah. All the kids."

"Oh, yeah. I went to a costume party at a bar on the coast. It got a little wild. A lot of fun, though."

Claire clicked her tongue. "You'll never get any candy that way."

"Liquor is quicker," Tammy laughed. "Trust me on this."

Claire went into her office, Tammy trailing behind her.

"So what did you do Saturday night?" she asked Claire.

"Manned the bowl for the trick-or-treaters."

Tammy visibly shuddered. "Children."

"You want children someday, don't you?"

Tammy gave her a look of mock-horror. "Bite your tongue! I don't plan on even thinking about kids for at least ten more years."

"Old mom," Claire teased.

"Not that old, girl. I'm only a couple of years older than you. Besides, are you looking to push a stroller?"

Claire tamped down the answer that wanted to spring forth. Yes, she wanted a child. And not in ten years. But with her job and with Cally, she didn't stand a chance of putting things in order before that could happen.

"Someday," was all she'd admit.

Tammy just shook her head. "I'm so not even thinking about it." She glanced at her watch. "I have an appointment in thirty minutes and I have to prepare. Do you want to get lunch together today?"

Claire held up her tote, which held her tablet and her lunch bag. "Brought something."

Tammy rolled her eyes dramatically. "Fine, fine. You brought something. I'll see you later."

"Yep."

Claire set her things down and booted up her computer. She'd left everything in order on Friday afternoon, as usual, but she still scrolled through the more recent docs added to the active account folders.

Inevitably, she came across the file she'd forwarded to herself after her meeting with Jake at the End Zone. And also inevitably, she thought about their pool games that night.

She'd liked kicking his ass, truth be told. He wasn't a sore loser, either. Not to mention the way he'd watched her as she'd played the table. Now, after his confession Saturday night, she knew all the delicious things he'd been thinking during their pool game.

"Good morning, Claire." Rick Chapman leaned into her office. "What's up?"

The hairs on the back of her neck stood at attention. Turning slowly in her chair, she faced Jake's brother. He wore a look of expectant smugness, if that could be a thing.

"Hi, Rick. Nothing much."

Rick smiled then. An easy expression that lit his whole face. "You don't have to hide it, Claire. I think it's great."

"W-what's great, exactly?"

"You and Jake."

Claire's mouth dropped open. "Me and… What are

you talking about?"

Rick held up a hand. "Okay, okay. I'm not teasing you, I swear." He glanced somewhere behind him in the hallway, and his smile grew wider. "Hey there, bro."

Claire's stomach tumbled down to her toes. Jake was here. Jake was here and his brother knew she'd slept with him.

"Good morning, sunshine." Jake all but pushed Rick out of his way. "Where do you want to have lunch today?"

He looked good. His polo shirt fit just right and was nearly the same blue as his eyes. In a flash she imagined him as he'd been in her bed yesterday morning, though. Wearing nothing but that same easy smile.

"Lunch?" she asked.

"Yeah. That meal between breakfast and dinner?"

She mirrored his smile but she was sure hers didn't look as comfortable as his. Rick was still watching from out in the hall, after all.

"I guess anywhere would be fine."

"Good." He glanced into the hall and nodded. "See you later, bro." He looked back at her. "I have to go over the numbers with Mr. Forbes this afternoon, and since I want you to present them with me I thought we could go over what we're going to say too."

The prospect of a working lunch put her on a little bit steadier footing, even though it would be more than that. He'd insisted she meet with Mr. Forbes and she couldn't think of a decent excuse to avoid it.

"Okay."

He did that glance into the hall again, then stepped in and kissed her. "You look pretty today, Claire."

And then he was gone. She held a hand to her chest, breathing in his scent as she licked at his taste on her lips. So what, they were dating now?

"So what, you two are dating now?"

Claire jumped at the sound of Tammy's voice. The woman looked curious, and a bright sparkle glinted in her eyes.

"I guess so."

Tammy laughed. "You guess so?"

Claire's cheeks flamed. "Yes. We're dating."

"When did this happen?"

"I don't know. We've been together a few times but

207

this weekend we… We took it to the next level."

Tammy stepped in and shut the door, her eyes bright. "Spill."

Claire gave a vigorous shake of her head. "No way. Besides, it doesn't really matter. Jake isn't staying around Cypress once his courses are finished. This is just for now."

"Yeah, Harmony thought that about Rick and he's been here four years now."

Claire knew what she was saying but she and Jake were far from what Harmony and Rick were. "Jake is a globetrotter, Tammy. There's nothing that would get him to give that up to stay in boring little Cypress Corners."

Tammy winked. "I can think of one thing."

Claire shook her head. "No way."

"You know better than I do." Tammy stood and crossed to the door, then turned. "Just enjoy yourself for once, Claire? I don't know what puts that worried expression on your face once in a while, but I can't think of a hotter guy than Jake Chapman to make you forget about it for a while."

Claire stared at Tammy, who gave her a sweet and

genuine smile before leaving her office. Claire turned to stare out her window. Did anyone else besides Tammy see that worry Claire tried so hard to hide? Did Jake?

She couldn't think about that now. What she'd told Tammy was true. Jake wasn't meant for hearth and home and domesticity. He was fun and in-the-moment and she decided she'd enjoy him while he was here.

If he took her heart with him when he inevitably left, so be it. She'd lived without it for so long, she doubted she would even miss it.

***

Jake had a lot riding on today's meeting. And now that hurdle was passed he had the true go-ahead to start construction. He'd had Claire with him at the meeting, which was such a blessing. No one could deny his girl when she was talking numbers. She got that focused, intense expression that turned him on and he felt everyone in the room giving her their full attention. Not the attention he wanted to give her, but he saw that she was respected. Valued. He wondered if she realized that. She worked so hard all the time it seemed like she was always afraid of losing the position she'd earned.

In the end, having her in his corner felt like as big an accomplishment as getting her to date him. And admitting it in front of Rick and Tammy.

"Another glass?" he asked her, lifting the wine bottle on the table.

She shook her head. They were at the Clubhouse, where they'd had their first date, though that one hadn't gone as he'd hoped. This one was easier and she actually seemed to order what she wanted instead of rabbit food.

"I shouldn't." She wiped her lips and set her napkin aside. "This was just lovely, Jake."

"It's not pizza at your place, but it'll work."

She smiled. "You think so?"

He arched his brows. "Oh, yeah."

That pink blush he loved spread over her cheeks. "We'll just see."

He set his own napkin aside. "I foresee a very comfortable couch in our future."

Her eyes darted around the restaurant as she checked if anyone was paying them any attention, but he didn't miss the sparkle in them as well. This was all new for him. Usually he paid upfront for his fun, dinner before going back to the girl's place. He was doing that tonight, but this didn't feel like those one-nighters. Claire was different. The fact that he'd spent the entire night with her Saturday was all the proof he needed to recognize that fact.

He paid the check and escorted her out to his waiting Jeep. Holding open the passenger door, he let her climb in then walked around to the driver's side.

"I'm going to drive you home, Claire."

She swallowed audibly and turned slightly toward him. "Yes, you are."

"And I'm going to come inside."

She nodded, heat coming into her blue eyes.

He resisted stating everything else he was going to do to her just as soon as he got her home. There was no need, really.

They pulled up and by the time they took the short walk to her door he was half-hard. The way this girl affected him was something he'd never encountered before.

He didn't miss that she trembled a little as she set her purse on the counter. Stepping behind her, he lifted her hair off the back of her neck and kissed her behind the ear. The soft sigh she gave stroked over him like a caress.

She leaned back against him. "Jake."

"Yeah, baby?" His tongue snaked out to tease her earlobe. "What do you want?"

She turned and stared up at him. "You. On the couch."

He smiled and kissed her lips. "I'm at your command."

Her eyes lit and he never saw anything hotter than Claire wanting him. Right now.

She grabbed his hand and they settled on what was quickly becoming his favorite piece of furniture. He sat and drew her down to straddle him. Her body was hot against him even through his pants and hers and he couldn't help but moan. Arching slightly, he ground up against her as he held her close.

"You set me on fire, Claire." He kissed her cheek, her throat, as he unbuttoned and peeled the blouse off of her. "So hot."

She pulled his shirt up and over his head, then kissed

him right over his heart. Reaching for his belt, she cupped his erection. Her fingers caressed him through his chinos and he moaned again.

"You're hard as a rock."

He could only nod. She gave him a tantalizing squeeze, then climbed off him just long enough to get rid of her pants before bringing her nearly-naked body up against his. Her skin was silk beneath his hands as he ran them over her. Warm and smooth and soft. Easing her bra strap down, he kissed her heated skin, right over her collarbone.

"Sweet Claire." He pushed the cups of her bra aside and stroked and kneaded her beautiful breasts. "So pretty."

She murmured something as he closed his mouth around one pert nipple and ran her fingers through his hair, holding him in place. There was no need. He could suck her breasts all day, she tasted so good.

Her body writhed against him then, and she had her fingers wrapped around him in the next second. "I want you inside me," she whispered, pulling back to stare at him.

He never would have thought she'd take control but that look of determination was on her beautiful face again. That focus that nearly made him come all over her hands.

"Condom," he rasped, thrusting up against her belly. "In my front pocket."

With a few economical motions she had him sheathed. Coming up on her knees, she pushed aside her panties and slid down onto him. She was tight and hot and held him just right.

"Christ!" he bit out.

He groaned as she took all of him. She started the rhythm and he silently vowed to hold on for as long as he could. She made these hot, purring sounds as she rode him. Closing his mouth around one of her nipples again, he bit and sucked as those sounds got louder.

"Oh, my!" She hurried her pace, then shuddered. "Oh, Jake!"

She came and he held on to her hips as he exploded inside her. Holding her against him, he placed little kisses against her dewy skin. He had her all over him.

Cradling her head, he stroked her hair. "God, I love

this couch."

She laughed softly, a relaxed sound she rarely made, and wrapped herself around him. He might be new to this dating thing, but if he was the one to make her lose herself like this he'd do just about anything to keep this going.

Chapter 17

"Oh, Claire!"

The singsong call made Claire squeeze her eyes shut and pray for escape from Lettie. Over the past week, the subject of her and Jake's dating seemed to be everywhere. Tammy was smugly happy for her and at dinner at the Chapman family's on Sunday night Harmony had looked like she was ready to order her maid of honor dress any day now. That was so not going to happen, since what she and Jake had was… She wasn't quite sure of what they had at the moment. That was the crux of it, then. An in-the-moment relationship, if that was a thing. That was new to her, but she figured that was about right.

Taking a breath, she ran her hands over her beige cardigan and turned to Lettie. "Hey there, Lettie."

The older woman grinned, reaching to tap the seat beside her. "Come and sit, Claire. I think we have some catching up to do."

Claire shrugged. "I don't know what you're talking about."

Lettie laughed. "Oh, you're a sly one! Although I'd

want to keep such a piece of delicious gossip under wraps, too."

Claire stared into Lettie's kind face, then sat down across from her. "It's not gossip, Lettie. Jake and I are dating."

Lettie crossed her arms on the table and leaned toward her. "Very nicely done. He's a catch."

"He may be a catch but he's not a keeper. Purely a catch-and-release kind of guy."

Lettie shook her head, her silver bangs brushing back and forth. "I don't know about that. He's been doing all that work on that adventure thing-a-ma-jigger. He's been squiring you all over the place. He's been palling around with his brother and taking care of that adorable little Nick."

"So what?"

Lettie's eyes grew round. "So what? He's putting down roots, Claire. That's what."

A foolish little bit of her heart gave a tiny jump at Lettie's words but the rest of it knew better.

"I don't think so," Claire said. "Jake's work takes him all over the globe. He would never stay here for more than a visit after his work is complete."

"Hmm, I don't know about that."

"I do. And I'm okay with that."

"I wouldn't be. Letting a pretty guy like that go?"

Claire stood. "I'm not the clinging type, Lettie. I have enough to worry about without scheming to keep my boyfriend around."

"Boyfriend?"

"What should I call him?" She raised her brows. "Lover?"

Lettie laughed as Claire had hoped. "Oh, you're a naughty girl, Claire Callahan!"

For once Claire didn't even care if the people sitting out on the patio heard Lettie. The woman was incorrigible so why fight it?

"Have a good day, Lettie."

Lettie waved a hand. "And you have a good night."

Shaking her head, Claire walked back to her office. Her work week was nearly over and then she could focus on having Jake all to herself. For the moment.

***

Jake collapsed on top of her, obviously spent. She

218

loved the feel of his body on top of hers, especially since he'd just given her two of the best orgasms she'd had to date. The smell of him, the feel of his skin, made her long to just let herself drift on the lingering sensations tingling over her body.

"You wore me out, Claire. After the week I've had, this just about did me in."

She smiled as he eased to one side and she watched him. "Jake Chapman, you're not saying I'm too much to handle?"

He laughed, deep and husky, and opened his eyes. "Just about, baby."

Grinning, she turned to prop herself up on an elbow. "So tell me about this week you've had."

"The grading and prep is nearly finished, thank God."

Claire nodded. "Tammy told me as much. What about your orders? On schedule?"

"For the most part. I'll have to go up to Orlando on Monday to kick some ass in gear. We'll have the footings done before the end of next week, so I have to make sure the posts for the apparatus will be delivered by then."

"It's going to be amazing, Jake."

"I hope so."

She saw a flicker of worry on his face, something she'd never seen before. He was usually the picture of confidence.

"You'll have to take me out to the site soon. I'd love to see what you're doing."

His eyes lit. "You'll love it. I know you can envision the big picture, along with all the little details."

She certainly saw the confidence he had in her. It did a lot for a girl's ego, that obvious faith. "Just say when."

"How about tomorrow?"

"Sure, I'd..." Damn. She had to see Cally tomorrow. "I can't tomorrow."

"Oh. What are you up to?"

Holding the sheets up to cover herself, she came to a sitting position. "I go see my father on Saturdays."

His brows rose. "I didn't know that. Every Saturday?"

She nodded. "He lives over in St. Cloud. In that fifty-five plus community over on one-ninety-two."

"I'll just have to entertain myself until your visit is

220

over. How long will you be there?"

"I'm not sure. I usually take him somewhere. Maybe we'll go walk around Old Town Village."

"That place with the quirky shops and rides and stuff?"

"And old-fashion arcade. That's Cally's favorite. Cally, that's my dad. Joseph Callahan."

"I'd love to meet him someday."

That shocked her. Jake wanted to meet Cally? They weren't a meet-the-parents type of couple, were they?

"Maybe," was all she'd say.

"You know Claire, I don't know anything about your family."

"You know everything now. Cally is all I have."

He gave a slow nod. "You lost your mom."

"Yes. It's been about five years ago now. Breast cancer."

"I'm sorry. Mine died when I was twelve. A heart thing."

"So your dad raised you?"

Jake laughed but the sound wasn't warm at all. "Hardly. Bill threw money at us and sent us to the best schools. I have to give him that, if nothing else."

Claire knew there had to be more to the story, but she wasn't going to pry. The last thing she would want was for anyone to know about her father's weakness and her crushing responsibilities because of it.

"You're close to your brother," she said. "That must be wonderful. I miss having a brother or sister."

"We have a sister. Cassie."

"That's right. I think I've heard Rick talk about her a couple of times. Where is she now?"

"Who the hell knows? The kid likes to travel and party, so she's currently running wild all over Europe."

Concern was etched on his face and she reached out to stroke his arm. "You miss her."

"I miss family, Claire. I'm loving being down here with Rick and my nephew."

"You'll miss them when you go."

It was a flat statement but he didn't deny it. They both knew he would go when the adventure courses were up and running.

"Yeah." He lifted a lock of her hair and rubbed it between his fingers, a soft smile on his lips. "They're not all I'll miss."

She looked down, knowing she would be unable to hide what his words made her feel. She would miss him, too.

"Hey, I can come back to visit." Jake kissed her. "As often as I can."

She just nodded. If that's what this was, a convenient relationship that was on and off, she would just go with it. She was in no position to hope for more, and she didn't have the time or energy to devote to it.

"Sure," she said brightly. "So, where are you taking me tomorrow night?"

He blinked at the quick change of subject, then grinned. "Anywhere you like. Maybe out on the coast?"

"Mmm." She cuddled against him and let the rise and fall of his chest distract her. "Sounds good."

He murmured something as he stroked her hair, and she took it to mean tenderness. That was all he offered her and it would have to be enough.

***

Claire parked her Prius beside the T-bird and got out. As she stepped up to Cally's screen door, she caught the tail end of his phone conversation.

"That's the one. Yeah. I'm all in."

Her heart dropped to her stomach. All in? Was he gambling again?

She rapped on the door. "Dad?"

Her father's smiling face filled the screen door. "Claire-bear!" He hung up on his call and placed the phone back in the cradle. "Come in!"

"Am I interrupting something?"

"What, the call? No. Barry just called and asked me what kind of pizza I wanted tonight."

She guessed that made sense. His bright eyes and innocent expression made it seem like he was being truthful. She'd seen enough of his act to know it wasn't always on the up and up, though.

"Pizza?"

"Yep. They order in but sometimes on Saturday I'm too stuffed from wherever you and I go to slap on the feedbag."

Laughing softly, she shrugged. "You might be hungry tonight, then. I thought we'd head over to Old Town Village and hit the arcade. They have the vintage car show there this weekend, too."

"That's right!" Cally rubbed his hands together. "We haven't gone there since last winter."

"I thought you'd like it."

They stepped outside and he clicked his tongue at her car. "Let's take the Thunderbird, Claire. You can drive."

Her heart raced as she imagined herself behind the wheel. Her sensible-shoe car just stared at her with its half smile while the T-bird seemed to grin at her in encouragement.

"Okay."

Cally brightened and she used the key on her ring. Sliding behind the wheel, she let her hands caress the tan leather seats for a minute.

"You look good sitting there, Claire." Cally got in and clicked his seatbelt, then tapped the dashboard. "Now, let's roll."

She backed out and they set off. The ride would take about half an hour. A few minutes in, Cally insisted they put the top down and she couldn't resist the notion. It was cooler now, and the breeze freed some hair from her ponytail to blow around her face. Cally leaned back, a look of pride on his face. Pride for his car and pride for his daughter. She knew how he loved her. That was never in question. It was nice to see the evidence of it today, though.

"You should take this car back to Cypress with you, Claire. It's made for you. The color and all."

"Not with my hair."

"Don't be silly. Your mother had the same beautiful hair and she looked good in everything."

Claire nodded. "Mom was a beauty."

"And so are you."

She glanced at him and smiled. "Thanks for saying that."

"I'm not just saying it. It's true. So tell me what's been going on with you."

She thought about Jake and their disclosures last night. Maybe she could share a little bit of that honesty with her father.

"I'm seeing someone."

"Yeah?" Cally straightened. "Is he good enough for you?"

"Oh, he's good enough for anybody."

"Hmm."

She glanced at him again. "What's that mean?"

"Who is this guy, Claire?"

"His name is Jake Chapman and he's building adventure courses out at Cypress."

"What's an adventure course?"

"A fitness course with obstacles and climbing walls and bridges. It's going to be amazing and there will be something for the kids, too."

"Sounds interesting. Your boss is on board?"

"Yes. It can only make money for their investors."

"And more money for you to count. That's good."

"Yes, it is."

Cally grew quiet and Claire let the drive take over her. Driving this car was intoxicating, even if it clashed with her coloring. It was beautiful, though. And by the interested looks a carload of guys gave her at a red light, maybe it didn't clash all that much. Maybe she'd start wearing her favorite color now and then. Maybe accessories at least. She had a few things in her closet in just this shade.

227

They arrived at Old Town Village and were directed to the place the show cars were parked. Cally said to take the special treatment so she parked the T-bird between a sixty-four Mustang and a Charger done up like the General Lee. She put up the top and locked it up tight.

They could hear the fifties music playing from the concourse of the village, and she grinned at her father.

"Now let's go play some Skee-ball."

"Skee-ball?" He laughed. "Claire-bear, you're on."

She put aside the strange sensation she'd had when she'd overheard that bit of his phone conversation and focused on a day spent having fun with her dad.

Chapter 18

"So what's Claire up to today?" Rick asked as he took a few burgers off the grill.

"She's spending the day with her dad."

"I think she does that every Saturday," Harmony put in, sitting across from Jake at the table.

She poured a cup of juice for Nick, who was playing with his trucks on the grass as usual. The kid looked extra cute today in his hooded sweatshirt emblazoned with the Cypress Institute's logo.

"That's what she told me. What's up with him?"

Harmony shrugged. "I'm not sure. He has a problem with his eyes. Or one eye. Macular Degeneration. So he can't work."

"She supports him," Jake stated.

Harmony's brows rose. "I guess that makes sense. She never treats herself to anything."

Jake nodded. "She is frugal, but I figured that was because she worked with numbers all the time. Now I get it."

"She's amazing with numbers." Rick set the platter of burgers on the table and sat. "We've been very happy with her."

"But is she happy?" Jake wondered aloud.

"What do you mean?" Harmony asked.

"I can't put my finger on it, but she seems so…cautious."

"She's dating you," Rick said. "She can't be that cautious."

Jake smirked at his brother. "Ha. Very funny. I mean in everything else, bro."

Harmony seemed to think for a long minute, then nodded. "I don't know what happened before she came to Cypress, but she was very closed-off when she first got here. Even I couldn't get her to do anything but work and go straight home every night."

"I think Nick wore her down," Rick said.

Jake smiled. "That's no surprise."

Harmony gazed at her son and smiled. "I admit I used him to ask Claire repeatedly to join us for dinner. My little monster did the trick."

Jake laughed. "Hey, Nick!"

"Yeah, Uncle Jake?"

"Do you like Claire?"

"Sure." He jumped up and ran over to the table. "Why? Is she coming? Is she bringing cookies?"

"No, honey," Harmony said. "She's busy today."

"Oh. Maybe Uncle Jake could get some of her cookies tonight and bring me some."

"You're half right," Rick said.

Jake shot him another look and took a bite of his juicy burger.

"How's the construction going?" Rick asked.

"Good." Jake wiped his mouth. "The footings are ready and everything's on track."

"When do you think it will be done?"

"In plenty of time for the New Year's opening."

"That's fast," Harmony said.

"A lot of the structure is pre-built. The rope bridges will need to be assembled, though. That will take time."

"And the rock-climbing wall?"

"That's pre-fab. The one for the kids, too."

"The kids?" Nick piped up. "When can I play on it?"

"Once it's done and certified safe, bud," Jake told him. "You can be the first kid to try it out."

Nick beamed at him. "Me? Yay!"

"Yay, indeed," Harmony said.

"Worried, sis?" Jake asked. "Don't be. I'd never hurt a hair on this little guy's head."

He ruffled Nick's hair for effect and the little boy giggled. Harmony's brow furrowed and she shared a look with Rick. Trepidation began to swirl in Jake's belly.

"What?"

Rick nodded and Harmony smiled at Jake.

"I know I probably shouldn't say anything. Claire's a big girl and can handle her own life."

"What are you saying, Harmony?" Jake asked.

"I just don't want you to hurt her."

Jake blinked rapidly. "I would never hurt her."

"You might not mean to, but come on," his brother said.

"We've had this conversation, bro." Jake took a breath to calm the irritation churning inside. "And Harmony, I know Claire is your friend. She's mine too, and I really like her."

Harmony opened her mouth, then shut it with a snap. She held her hands up in apparent surrender. "I believe you, Jake. I won't say anything more about it."

"Good." He bent down and grabbed Nick up in his arms. "Now how about we go for a walk down on the dock, Nick? I'll show you where the kids' course is going to be."

"Honey?" Rick asked.

Harmony waved a hand. "Go. I'll clean up."

Rick gave her a kiss, a bend-her-over-one-arm-and-kiss-the-daylights-out-of-her kiss, and straightened. "You're the best."

"Yeah, yeah." Harmony kissed Nick's cheek, then waved her hands at her flushed cheeks. "Boys."

Jake and Rick both laughed as they each took one of Nick's hands and led the way to the dock. Jake couldn't help thinking about what Harmony and Rick said, though. He didn't want to hurt Claire. He liked spending time with her and loved getting as close as he could, too. She seemed to like what they had going on right now. Did she want more?

It didn't matter. More wasn't in the cards for him. That prospect was as foreign as his sister Cassie's favorite club of the moment.

***

233

Claire stood in front of her closet, trying to decide what to wear for her date with Jake. They were going out to the coast, so a pair of tan skinny jeans and a scoop-neck top would work topped with one of her ever-present cardigans. She pulled on the jeans and stood there in her bra debating shirt and sweater combinations. God, she was so boring.

A flash of poppy orange caught her eye then. It was the sweater she'd treated herself to at the mall in Orlando a few weeks ago. She picked it up. It was soft and had the sweetest little pearl buttons. Turning to the mirror hanging on the back of the closet door, she held the sweater up to her freckled face.

"Not totally frightening," she said to herself.

With one hand she swept her hair to rest it over one shoulder on top of the sweater. Instead of the cringe-worthy orange nightmare she'd expected her hair looked lustrous against the knit. Smiling at her reflection, she grabbed a white t-shirt with a deep V and tugged it on. Shrugging into the sweater, she smoothed it and checked herself again.

"Not bad." She rummaged through her jewelry

drawer for the chunky necklace she'd bought on that same trip, a collection of different-sized faux stones in varying shades of her favorite color. It would drape beautifully above the neckline of her shirt and was the perfect touch.

Sliding on a pair of flats, she left her room to wait for Jake. She didn't have to wait long. He rang the bell right when he'd texted her he would. Six on the dot.

She pulled the door open and found herself gazing at his backside. Not that he didn't have a great backside but she tapped him on the shoulder anyway. He started, then turned to her with a grin.

"Man, that car is gorgeous."

She saw he was eyeing the T-bird. "Yeah. It's my dad's but he can't drive anymore. I took him to Old Town Village in it and he insisted I drive it home after."

He looked at the car again, then back at her. "You drove that? That is so hot."

She smiled up at him. "Yeah? Better than my boring old Prius?"

"Oh, yeah." He finally stepped into the house and wrapped his arms around her. "I think I want to fool

235

around with you in that T-bird."

At the moment she could envision making out with him on the soft tan leather seats. The image made her chuckle.

"There's very little room in that car, Jake."

He dropped his hands to her butt and pulled her close against him. "Then we'll have to settle for your bed or the climax couch."

She laughed. "Climax couch?"

"What would you call it?"

"I don't know, but I won't be able to look at it the same way ever again."

The heat in his eyes told her he was thinking about every delicious thing they'd done on that couch, up to and including the night she took charge for once.

Pulling back, she pressed her hands against her flaming cheeks and cleared her thoughts. "You ready to go?"

"Sure." He stepped out onto the porch again. "We're so taking the T-bird."

"Okay." They walked to the car and Claire dug in her purse. "You drive."

Jake's brows rose, then he took the keys from her hand. "Whatever the lady wants."

Oh, he could make anything sound naughty.

He held her door open and she slid inside. When he got behind the wheel, he took a minute to just stroke the steering wheel.

"Do you two want to be alone?" she asked.

He barked out a laugh and shook his head, then gave her another hot look. "Just sit back, baby. I'm driving."

He started the car, which purred under his touch. Just like every female in a ten-mile radius.

"Top down?"

She nodded. "Sure. Why do I care what my hair looks like."

He pressed the button then leaned back and ran his gaze over her hair. "Your hair is gorgeous, Claire. And with you wearing the same color as this pretty car? Let's just say I'm going to have a boner the whole way to the coast."

She grinned and settled back as he pulled away from the curb.

As the miles between Cypress Corners and

237

Melbourne Beach sped past, Claire felt a niggling of
unease in her belly. She hadn't been back since the big
move three years ago. Not since going through her dad's
things and finding little of value tucked away in the home
he'd lost. She hadn't had many friends out here before
then anyway. Not with working long hours to put herself
through classes at the community college and then
driving back and forth between Melbourne and the
University of Central Florida both to complete her
bachelor's degree in accounting and her MBA before
sitting for CPA exam. School and work. That had been
her life while her dad was throwing away all the money
her mom had managed to squirrel away from her dad's
addiction before her death.

"Hey, you're quiet."

Jake's voice reached her but she kept her gaze on the
cattle dotting the wide expanse of ranchland they passed.

"Just thinking."

More silence between them. "How was your father?
Did you have a good time?"

She finally turned her head to stare at his profile.
"Old Town Village is always fun. They have a classic

cars show almost every weekend, and dad just ate that up."

"Maybe you and I can drive out there next weekend. They have rides and things, right?"

"They have zip lines and these rides that strap you in and shoot you up and around like a slingshot."

Jake threw her a smile. "That sounds like fun."

"To you, maybe."

He shrugged. "I can't talk you into letting me strap you in, Claire?"

Her body tingled a little but she knew he was just teasing to bring her out of her quiet funk. It was working. That was for sure.

"Depends on the incentive, Jake. What's in it for me?"

He raised his brows and looked both silly and sexy. She shook her head and just smiled.

"Where to?" he asked as they were just a couple of miles from the city. "You're from here, right?"

"Yes, but I haven't been back in a while. You pick."

"Why don't we drive down the intracoastal and eat on the river?"

"Sounds good."

Jake soon pulled the T-bird into the parking lot of a quirky little shack-looking place set right on the water. The lot was pretty full but he didn't look bothered by it as he put the top back up.

It looked like a few parties were waiting to be seated but Jake went right up to the hostess stand and gave the girl working it his brightest smile.

"May I help you?" the girl asked, her eyes wide.

"Looks like you're pretty busy, but I wondered if there was anything outside?"

She flushed and ruffled through the papers on the stand. "Out on the deck is first-come, first-serve, but... There might be... Um, how many?"

Jake's smile widened and Claire felt it all but bounce off the girl's face. "Two."

She nodded and grabbed two menus from the stand. "I'm taking this couple out on the deck, Diane." She said to a server standing there. She eyed Jake again. "Follow me."

Claire wondered if the hostess had even seen her, but Jake took Claire's hand and drew her ahead of him.

"After you," he said.

The hostess showed them to a small table set in one corner of the deck. The view was gorgeous and Claire waited for the girl to give up the menus. And the hopeful expression she kept trained on Jake's face.

"Thanks," Jake said.

The hostess finally left them and Claire ran her fingers through her hair. "I must look lovely."

Jake turned all that masculine attention on her now. "You do."

It was breezy out here on the river but that wasn't the reason for the shiver that ran through Claire's body. She grabbed up a menu and focused on the restaurant and the company. She was sitting at a table with a great view, both over the river and across the table. And afterwards Jake would drive her back to her house in the Thunderbird and give her his special brand of attention all night long. She had no doubt about that. Tomorrow was Sunday, so she would just sleep until he tickled her awake like last week.

She'd put the memories of Melbourne and the worries about her father out of her mind and choose to live in the moment. And when a moment was this sweet, how could she not?

She'd just pray that, when the moment passed, she would be able to move on and go back to her safe, boring life.

Chapter 19

Jake hoisted the post into position, holding it steady as Jim placed and tightened the braces attaching it to the concrete footing. He nodded at Jim and straightened, reaching overhead to stretch his back. The physical exertion felt good, after the past few days of spending too much time in his head. Even with his daily runs and laps in the pool, he still couldn't just get his thoughts off the path they'd been running down since dinner with Claire on Saturday night.

Spending most of the weekend with her had been an eye-opener. It was actually fun to wake up with a woman after loving her all night. They'd spent Sunday together and even gone shopping at a flea market that afternoon. Claire was very frugal with her money. He'd known that. But to watch her worry over every little purchase she was considering for herself as if she didn't think she deserved it? That struck him as sad and a waste of time. She was worth it, in his opinion. She was worth everything.

And that was the thought that threw him face first into his work this week. Hard. He was out of Cypress when the courses were up and ready. By the New Year

he'd be back in Boston and mapping out his next
assignment. And there would be a next assignment, no
matter what his father had said in his latest phone call.
The old man wanted him to stick around for a while.
Work at headquarters with him. That was so not
happening. No fucking way.

"Jake!"

As if summoning Bill Chapman with his dark
thoughts, there the man stood just a few feet away. Hands
held tight at his sides as he eyed the work in progress that
would be part of the adventure courses. Jake looked back
at the footings he and the men had placed today and
figured if anyone could find fault with the project's
growth it was his father.

"Dad." Jake took off his work gloves and brushed
his hands over his jeans. "What brings you here?"

Bill eyed Jake, from his earring to his muddy work
boots, then met his gaze. "Tiffany was getting tired of the
cold up in Boston, so I thought we'd combine business
with pleasure. We're here for a long weekend."

Jake inwardly cringed. His stepmother was a piece
of work. A man-eater of the first order and, despite the

obvious effort she put into her upkeep, she was rapidly becoming a cougar on the prowl. God, he didn't want to think about the last time he'd seen her.

She'd come into his office, with her usual low-cut blouse and skirt slit up one thigh. She'd teased him about his new assistant, and asked how long he was going to wait until he fucked her. Lovely woman, his stepmother. He didn't want to think about her at all but especially not today.

It was bright and sunny here in Florida, the November air holding a freshness that wouldn't turn chilly for a couple more weeks. He just wanted to finish his day at the work site and go back to his tent-cabin with his muscles humming and his mind quiet. Maybe he'd bring Claire out to his place this time. That bed was cozy and soft, and she would look amazing spread on the well-worn quilt. Bill was staring at him expectantly though, so he knew there was no true escape.

"How is dear old step-mom?"

Bill's brows knocked together, then he waved a hand. "She's at the spa, then she's going shopping in Orlando."

"No doubt." Jake stepped over the tape marking the edge of the path. "What do you want?"

"Can't I just visit my son at his work site?"

"Can you? Yes. Are you? Doubtful."

Bill nodded. "Fine, fine. I have a meeting with Forbes this afternoon and I wanted you there."

"Me? What the hell for?"

"I want to drive home the fact that this project is going to make money for everyone involved. Can you get the little redhead to join us?"

"Us? I'm not going to that meeting with you." He chose to ignore the question about Claire. He'd never drag her into a meeting with Bill.

"Why the hell not?" his father asked.

"Because I have work to do, Dad. Actual work to make sure this project is finished on time and making money sooner rather than later."

"Admirable," Bill said. "You can skip the meeting. Tammy will be there. And she'll get the money girl there, too."

Jake's stomach twisted as he pictured Claire shut in a room with Bill, but at least Tammy and Mr. Forbes would be there as buffers. "Okay, then."

"We're eating at the Clubhouse tonight, Jake. I expect you there."

"Why?"

"Tiffany wants a family dinner out. And your brother..." Bill's cheeks turned ruddy. "Rick's busy."

Yeah. Busy avoiding the hell out of Bill and his particular brand of crap.

"He has a life, Dad. A busy job and a family."

"Yeah." Bill eyed the ground. "How's Nick?"

"Great. Nick's an amazing kid."

Jake saw regret on his father's face and, for a second, he seemed like a human being. Then his blue eyes narrowed and he waved a hand. "So I'll see you at the restaurant at seven."

Jake knew an order when he heard one. He could flip his father the finger and tell him to fuck off or he could suck it up and sit through one dinner like a big boy.

"Sure." Jake let out a breath. "Seven."

Besides, if he placated Bill maybe the man wouldn't bug Rick and Harmony on this trip. Dinner would keep Tiffany out of Rick's hair, anyway. She'd be happy enough grabbing Jake's thigh under the table as she asked questions dripping with double-entendre. She spoke it like a second language.

"That's fan-fucking-tastic," Jake grumbled.

"What's that, boss?" Jim called.

Jake smiled at him. "Just thinking about my dinner plans, Jim."

Jim stared at him for a beat. "Oh."

He went back to tightening the bolts on the braces and Jake walked over to help him.

***

Claire sat at her desk, going over the notes she'd taken at the afternoon's impromptu meeting. She'd been dragged into the meeting with Mr. Forbes and Tammy, and she'd been surprised to see Bill Chapman there too. She'd never met him before but she would have known Jake and Rick's father anywhere. The same broad shoulders. The same stunning blue eyes. There was a weariness in Bill's eyes, though. Something she never saw in his sons'. The man wasn't happy, but with his booming voice and take charge personality she figured he thought no one would notice.

"So are you going to go to dinner?" Tammy asked.

Claire turned. "Do you think I could back out now? I still can't believe Mr. Chapman invited me."

"Are you surprised? Mr. Forbes told him you were dating Jake. You can't get out of it now."

"No. I don't think he's a man who likes to be refused."

Tammy laughed. "Nope. Just wait until you meet the missus."

"He didn't mention his wife would be there. What's she like?"

Tammy came into the office and sat on the edge of Claire's desk. "Tiffany Chapman is a piece of work. And I mean carefully-orchestrated-plastic-surgery piece of work. She's a bitch, too."

"Tammy!"

"She is. Just ask Rick."

"Just ask me what?"

Rick leaned into the office with a curious expression.

"Hey, Rick. I'm going to dinner tonight with Jake and your dad."

Rick frowned. "Yeah, Bill's here. He contacted me

this morning."

"How come you get out of dinner?" Claire asked.

Rick didn't even crack a smile at her teasing. "Bill and I don't talk much, Claire. There's no way in Hell I'm going to share a meal with him and Tiffany."

"Oh." Claire sighed. "He knows I'm dating Jake."

Rick's brows rose. "I don't envy you tonight. My stepmother is going to have a field day with that information."

"Yeah, I told her Tiffany's a bitch." Tammy whispered the last word this time.

"Good. Take Tammy's word for it, Claire. I'd warned Harmony before the one and only night we had dinner with them and she thought I was exaggerating. Until she met Tiffany."

"I'm a little frightened now," Claire said.

"You'll have Jake there with you," Rick said. "My brother won't let her get away with anything tonight."

Claire swallowed and glanced over at Tammy. Her friend was nodding slowly, backing up everything Rick said.

"You'll have to give me the rundown tomorrow

morning," Tammy said.

Claire told her she would and Tammy and Rick left her to her thoughts. And her worries. She was having dinner with Jake's father and stepmother. Her friends warned her how awful it would be and she really had no way to get out of it. She'd just concentrate on Jake and hope the evening went quickly.

She parked the Prius in the lot at the Clubhouse, regretting again that she'd brought the Thunderbird back to Cally's place last night. She and Jake had made out a little in that car Saturday night, just like he'd promised. It had been hot and they'd barely managed to get into her house before doing every naughty thing Jake had whispered in her ear. He'd said since he'd driven the car he'd let her drive that night. And she had. She'd driven them both out of their minds.

Cally had looked surprised, but oddly pleased she'd returned the car. He'd been surprised she'd visited on a Wednesday, too. Said he had a standing date with his bingo buddies and he all but gave her the bum's rush. Still, the affection in his eyes had been as clear as always. Definitely different from the hard expression on

Bill Chapman's face that afternoon.

"Hi, Claire," the hostess, a girl she knew now, said as Claire stepped inside.

"Hey, Janie." Claire looked around, but didn't see the Chapmans. "I'm meeting some people for dinner."

"Yes, they're here." Janie stepped around the hostess stand. "I'll walk you over."

Claire's belly flipped and her heels clicked over the wood floor as she followed Janie to a table prominently set in the center of the restaurant. Claire had changed after work, and wore a knit dress in a soft shade of green. And some pretty underwear she hoped to show Jake later.

She spotted Bill Chapman where he was seated across from Jake. Jake didn't look happy to be there but as she came up to the table his eyes grew round.

"Claire?" He stood. "What are you doing here?"

"I invited her," Mr. Chapman said. "You two are dating, aren't you?"

"Dating?"

The question, asked in a singsong voice, drew Claire's gaze to the woman sitting next to Bill. Whoa. Expensive highlights and lowlights, pricey clothes, piercing gaze. This could only be the dreaded Tiffany.

"Hello," Claire said.

Jake stepped around the table and took her elbow. "Let's go."

"Jake, stay." Tiffany rested her folded arms on the table, hiking up her tanned cleavage. "We want to get to know your girlfriend."

Jake rolled his eyes, then smiled at Claire. "I'm sorry for this."

Claire stared into his beautiful eyes and couldn't help but tease him a little. "I'll let you make it up to me," she whispered.

He smiled but she could see the tension around his mouth. "Sit, please." He waved her into the chair beside his. "Claire, you know my father. This is Tiffany. His wife."

Claire nodded to Mr. Chapman and faced the probing look on his wife's face.

"So, you're the money girl Bill told me about?" she asked.

Claire nodded. "I'm the CPA, yes."

Tiffany waved a jeweled hand. She had a very nice

manicure, too. "Ugh, numbers. Counting money must be so boring."

"You like spending it," Mr. Chapman said.

Tiffany giggled, actually giggled. "Oh, Bill!"

The dinner went downhill from there. Jake answered in monosyllables to questions posed by both his father and his stepmother. That woman stared daggers at Claire as she picked at her food and drank deeply of the pricey wine Mr. Chapman ordered. Claire didn't have much of an appetite, either. Jake was a different person tonight. Stiff and stilted and his discomfort was a living thing. When she reached beneath the table to touch him he'd jumped before taking her hand in his.

"I wish your brother and his family could have joined us," Tiffany said as their plates were cleared. "But Rick is a busy boy."

Claire all but felt Jake flinch at her statement.

"Are you still staying with them?" his father asked.

Jake shook his head. "No. I'm out at the far lakeside."

"In the tent-cabin?" Tiffany smiled in Claire's direction. Her gaze sharpened. "Have you been out there

254

yet, Claire? It's very…cozy."

"When were you there?" Jake asked, then seemed to regret engaging the woman in conversation.

"When Rick was first down here," Tiffany answered. "Melody lived out there, right?"

"Harmony," Mr. Chapman corrected.

Jake seemed surprised by his father's contribution, but he turned to Claire. "Let's get out of here."

It was abrupt but Claire couldn't blame Jake if he was less than gracious. She felt like she'd been sitting on pins and needles all evening and was just as eager to leave as he appeared to be.

"Sure." Claire nodded to his father. "Thank you so much for dinner, Mr. Chapman." She stood and faced Tiffany. "It was very nice to meet you, Mrs. Chapman."

The woman's smile wasn't very friendly but her teeth were dazzling white. "Claire."

Jake's hand at Claire's back both reassured her and hurried her away from the table. He didn't say anything until they were outside, when he took a deep breath and ran his fingers through his hair.

"God, I'm so sorry." He touched her cheek, his

fingers gentle. "I didn't know he'd talked you into dinner."

"It was…nice."

Jake smiled at her. "It was so not nice, Claire. They both suck in their own unique ways."

"I hope I didn't intrude."

He stared at her, then laughed out loud. "That's what I needed. You intruding. You're the only thing that kept me from running screaming from the restaurant."

She took his hand in hers. "Let's go to your place, Jake. I hear it's very cozy."

He drew her close, bringing his lips to her temple. "You got it."

Chapter 20

Jake gripped the wheel of the Jeep as it bounced gently over the path toward the tent-cabin. His hands were clammy and his pulse still raced from holding everything back during dinner. A slight headache beat rhythmically between his eyes.

"I can't apologize enough for those two, Claire."

"It's okay, Jake. Besides, I was forewarned."

"What?" He glanced over at her. "Who warned you?"

"Tammy and your brother."

Jake nodded and faced forward again. "Yeah, they would both know. Rick all too well."

"Your father doesn't seem very happy."

"With Tiffany?" He snorted. "Shit, would you be?"

"No, but that's not what I mean. He just seemed a little put out when Tiffany was talking about Rick and Harmony."

"Melody," Jake said with a smile. "Like she doesn't know Harmony's name."

"She is a special kind of bitch," Claire said. "Rick was right on the money."

257

"The boring money?" Jake shook his head. "You weren't spared a barb or two tonight, either. Again, sorry."

She smiled at him, a beautiful smile that was a surprise and delight after the shitty dinner they'd just endured. It was easy to forget about his father and Tiffany when Claire looked at him like that.

He stopped the Jeep and pulled the brake. "Come on." He ran around to her side and opened her door. "As fun as making out in the T-bird was last Saturday, I don't want to do anything to scare the animals out here."

She laughed, free and easy, and he wanted nothing more than to lose himself in her. For a night. For a couple of weeks. For as long as he could manage before that itch came again and he had to get the hell out of Dodge.

Claire looked around the cabin as Jake lit a couple of lamps. The lighting was soft and warm and he couldn't wait to get her naked. He stepped up to her and pulled her close, breathing in her sweet scent as he let go of the tension. Another kind of tension curled through him, starting from every point of contact between her body and his.

"I love holding you," he whispered, running his hands over her.

She murmured something and stepped back. "Then let's get rid of these clothes."

He watched as she pulled that soft sweater dress thing up and over her head. She wore a bra and panties in what he thought of as her color now. That orange pink she looked so great in. Her skin was creamy-looking and his mouth watered.

"You look so good in that color, Claire."

She shook her head. "You're just thinking about the T-bird."

He laughed and shed his own clothes. "How about I let you drive again tonight?"

Taking her in his arms, he fell on the bed and ran his hands all over her warm, creamy skin. She kissed him and he gave her his tongue as she ground against him. Their underwear was suddenly in the way and he worked her bra free as she eased down the band of his boxer briefs.

She ground against his dick and his eyes nearly rolled back in his head.

"I have to get inside you," he bit out.

She pushed against his chest and leaned back, straddling his hips as she handled him.

"You're ready already?"

He groaned as she stroked him. "It doesn't take much to get me ready for you."

She flipped her hair back over one shoulder and smiled down at him. "Then let's do something about that."

She bent down and kissed his chest, her mouth closing over one of his nipples.

"In the nightstand, Claire."

He sucked in a breath as she eased off of him to stand beside the bed. She shimmied out of her panties and he nearly came just watching her. Reaching into the nightstand drawer, she pulled out a condom and tossed it his way. When she crawled back over him he knew he had to get some control or he was going to be very embarrassed in a few short minutes.

"Sorry, baby." He flipped her over. "You can drive next time."

She laughed and then let out a moan as his mouth

ran all over her. Her sweetness was everywhere. On her lips. On her breasts. Between her legs. He couldn't wait any longer.

He ripped open the condom wrapper and was inside her before another second passed. Moving faster and faster, he closed his eyes and let himself feel as she rose up to meet him thrust for thrust.

"Jake!"

She sobbed his name again as she came, and the sound was even sweeter than she was. A few more thrusts and Jake finally gave in, letting his climax tear through him as he held her as close as he could.

Her breath was still coming fast as he buried his face in the crook of her neck. After a few minutes he withdrew from her and grabbed the edge of the quilt, pulling it over the two of them.

"So do you like my cozy little tent-cabin?" he asked her.

She let out a purr and cuddled closer. "It's no climax couch, but it'll do."

He laughed and concentrated on just breathing in and out until he could rouse the strength to have her again.

***

The next morning Claire was humming to herself as she went into the coffee shop. Last night had been so strange. Strange and amazing. First the horrible dinner with the Chapmans and then the incredible night with Jake at his cabin. Cuddling with him on that iron bed was so wonderful. She could get used to that feeling. Being safe and warm. Secure. Like nothing could touch her.

She ordered and paid for her coffee and moved back to wait.

"Good morning, Claire."

She looked over to see Tiffany Chapman picking up her own cup of coffee at the end of the counter. "Good morning, Mrs. Chapman."

"Tiffany, please." She leaned closer. "You are sleeping with my stepson."

Claire's cheeks flamed but only part of it was embarrassment. How dare she say such a thing? "I'm not talking about this with you."

The other woman shrugged. "Suit yourself. I think it's sweet you want to protect Jake's reputation. You're such a sweet girlfriend." She clicked her tongue and shook her head. "If you only knew."

Claire's name was called, sparing her from continuing this horrid conversation. "Have a nice day, Mrs. Chapman."

Tiffany's eyes narrowed but Claire just walked past her out into the beautiful fall day. She knew what the woman was trying to do. Claire knew all about Jake's reputation. He was a lady's man and, after they were finished with whatever this was, he'd find another girl to sleep with. Pain stabbed at her stomach but she just ignored it and took her usual too-hot first sip of her latte.

She focused on her work and put Jake's stepmother out of her head. The woman really was a bitch, and Claire didn't want to spare her any more thought.

By the time her Friday was wrapping up, she'd input the numbers for the week and readied her desk for Monday. It was another weekend. Another Saturday with her father and another Saturday night with Jake. And hopefully another Sunday, too.

"You sticking around Cypress this weekend, Claire?" Tammy asked.

"Yep."

Tammy laughed. "I don't blame you. Even though the Chapmans will still be here."

"I'm not letting her get to me, Tammy. Nope."

"Good for you." Tammy waved. "I'll see you on Monday."

Claire shut down her computer and turned off her light.

"Heading out, Claire?" Mr. Forbes asked as she reached the lobby.

"Yes, sir. Have a nice weekend."

"You too."

When she got back to her house she wasn't surprised to see Jake's Jeep parked out front. Her heart did that silly skip thing as she turned off her ignition and climbed out. He was sitting on her porch. Looking like he belonged there. Like he would always be there. God, she was a fool.

"Hey, Jake."

He patted the chair next to him. "I thought we'd watch the sunset."

That was so sweet she nearly swooned. Oh, she knew what was going on with her lately. While he was having a good time she was busy falling in love. She had to get a grip and fast. She was an independent woman. She made her own money and her own decisions. She didn't need a man no matter how hot he was or how good he made her feel.

"Okay."

They sat in companionable quiet for a few minutes, then Jake turned to her. "Pizza?"

"Sure." She glanced at him, then noticed how tired he looked. There were shadows under his eyes. "Hey, are you okay?"

"Just beat. I worked my ass off today out at the courses."

"How's it coming?"

"The climbing apparatus are coming at the end of next week so we really need to make sure the sites are ready. The rope bridges are already being built, so it looks like we'll make it."

She wanted to ask if his father's visit had anything to do with his extra push to get things done, but didn't feel it was her place. Despite what Tiffany said, she wasn't his girlfriend. Not really.

265

"I'm sure you will."

He closed his eyes. "I could use a beer."

"Then you're in luck. I have a beer."

He peeped open one eye and smiled. A lazy smile that did wonderful things to his face and amazing things to her body.

"Then, let's go grab a couple and pick up the pizza on the way to the tent-cabin."

Oh, another cozy night. "Sounds like a plan."

Later that night, curled up in Jake's arms after their second time, she had to face facts. She was in up to her ears with this guy and there was no way she would ever let him know. He was rushing to get his project finished and then he'd leave. She wasn't melodramatic enough to think he was in a hurry because of her and what they had right now. But she had to admit that once he was done he was out of there. Before Christmas, which was what it was looking like now.

Another lonely holiday stretched out in front of her. Maybe a cookie exchange or two. Lonely Christmas Eve. Sad little dinner with Cally on Christmas Day. It was what she'd come to expect and she was an idiot for wanting anything more.

***

On Saturday morning Claire woke up to find herself alone in Jake's bed. Touching a hand to his pillow, she found it was still warm. She located her bra and panties but there was no way she was going to put her work clothes back on and do an official walk of shame this morning. Instead she grabbed a t-shirt from the desk chair and pulled it over her head. It smelled like Jake. Fresh and delicious.

The sunrise drew her out onto the little deck at the back of the tent-cabin, and she found Jake sitting in one of the Adirondack chairs. He wore a worn shirt and a pair of jeans but he was barefoot. The morning was dewy cool and the sunlight was pink and pretty stretching out over the lake, but he didn't appear to be enjoying it.

"Hey," she said softly.

He turned, then smiled as his eyes ran over her. "You look good in my shirt, Claire."

She pulled her hair over one shoulder and twisted it to give it some control, then settled down in the chair next to his. "Couldn't sleep?"

"Couldn't sleep in," he put in. "I have to go out to the site today."

"On a Saturday?"

"It has to get done and soon. I won't have Bill crowing about how I never finish anything I start."

Ouch. That came from somewhere deep inside him.

"I'm sure you'll finish on time."

"Ahead of time, if I can help it."

He seemed driven in that moment. Like a Jake she'd never seen before. His father's visit must have affected him a lot more than he would ever admit, but she wasn't going to press him to admit that. She had daddy issues of her own to deal with.

"If you'll take me back to the Clubhouse I can get my car and drive home."

He stood and shook his head. "No. I'll drive you home."

Why had she followed him there in the first place? Turned out she should have driven all the way out here, given his odd mood this morning.

"But I need my car, Jake. I'm going to see my father today."

He looked confused, then nodded. "Right. It's Saturday."

"Yeah."

"Why don't you get ready and we'll go. I have a pair of sweats you can put on."

There was a chill in his voice and she could almost feel him pushing her away. Where was the playful lover from last night? Where was the guy who always said the right thing and made her think she could have a little happiness once in a while?

Her moment was passed, then. He would finish this project, on time or sooner if he could help it, and leave Cypress Corners. And her, not that she had any hold on him. He'd said he'd be back now and then. She'd probably take him right back into her bed when he did, too.

The ride back to the Clubhouse was quiet with each of them lost in their own thoughts. Just how much longer did she have with him? A few weeks, if that.

He kissed her softly, though. Then made sure no one noticed her getting into her car looking like a bag lady before she drove back home. Her eyes burned with unshed tears that she couldn't allow. Who was she to cry over nothing? Over a non-breakup of a non-relationship? It was crazy.

After her shower and two cups of coffee, she felt like she could face the world. And her father. She drove into St. Cloud and when she got to Cally's the first thing she noticed was that the T-bird was gone.

Chapter 21

Bile rose in the back of Claire's throat as her head began to pound.

"What the hell?"

She got out of her car and mechanically climbed the steps, taking a calming breath before rapping on the screen door.

"Just a minute," her father said from inside.

Her heart raced as she stared at the spot where the Thunderbird usually sat. Nope. Her eyes weren't playing tricks on her. It was still empty. Deserted.

"Come on, Dad. Open up."

Cally opened the door and peered at her through the screen. "Hi, Claire-bear."

"Where is it?"

He blinked his big Callahan-blue eyes at her. "Where's what?"

"The car, Dad. The Thunderbird. Where the hell is it?"

He smiled at her, his eyes twinkling, but she saw a brittleness in his expression. "I had a bit of bad luck."

With those words, her heart fell to the concrete steps.

271

Clutching at the handrail, she struggled to remain upright as black dots swam into her field of vision.

"My God, Claire." He pushed open the screen door and grabbed her arm. "Come in, sweetheart."

She let him lead her into the mobile home, then collapsed onto the couch. "It's gone." She licked her parched lips. "A bit of bad luck."

"Now, I know if I have a stake I can get it back."

Claire buried her face in her hands, her eyes burning as tears seeped through her lashes. "A stake." She sucked in a breath and lifted her head to pin him with her stare. "A stake? Are you kidding me?"

He pulled back, holding up his hands. "I don't have any money, Claire. How am I supposed to play if I don't have any money?"

"Play what? Dad, what did you do?"

"Played a sure thing. Or thought I did."

"A sure thing?" Her voice had taken on a high, shrill quality that would probably shatter every window in every nearby mobile home. "You gambled? You're not supposed to gamble!"

"It was a sure thing."

He looked at her, his lower lip stuck out, and in that moment he looked like a recalcitrant little boy. A little boy who had cost her so much, who still cost her, and now had lost the one thing of value they had.

"Oh, Dad." She let the tears fall and let him see them for once.

"Don't cry, honey." He placed a hand on her shoulder. "I'll win it back. You'll see."

That did it. She rubbed at her cheeks with the heels of her hands and took in a soggy breath. "No, you won't. You're not going to do a damn thing."

"Now, Claire—"

"You've done enough!"

His mouth dropped open, then he nodded. "You're right."

"I'm right? That's all you have to say now?"

"I'm sorry, Claire. What else can I say?"

"Gee, I don't know Dad." She stood and began to pace the small space. "You're sorry. Where have I heard that before? Oh! From you! To Mom. To Me. About every single time you lost money. Lost the mortgage payment. Lost the utility payment. Lost your fucking bonus!"

He sank back into the couch, looking small and vulnerable. She so wanted to hold on to her anger. To be pissed and lash out at him for fucking up again and throwing away everything she worked for. An uneasy feeling tickled the back of her mind.

"Tell me the mobile home is safe."

"You hold the title and the deed, Claire-bear."

"And?"

"I can't touch it so I didn't. I swear."

"Okay. You've never lied to me so I guess that's something."

He nodded. "And I'll get the car back, sweetheart. I swear."

"Who has it?"

His eyes slid toward a corner of the living space.

"Dad." She stood in front of him, waiting for him to raise his head. When he did, she stared down at him. "Who has it."

"A guy out in Kissimmee. Runs one of the classic car shows."

"You met him at Old Town Village."

It wasn't a question and Cally didn't pretend to think about his answer. He just nodded again.

"I want his name."

"You can't contact him, Claire. What will he think?"

"I don't give a shit what he thinks, Dad. I want my car back."

"Your car?"

"Yes, my car. I love that car. I want it back. I should have changed the registration and title to my name when we left Melbourne."

"I earned that car."

"No. You won that car. Not gambling, for once in your life though. Still, it's mine now and I'm getting it back."

Cally stood, his shoulders slumped, and took out his wallet. Thumbing through the worn leather, he withdrew a business card. "The guy's name is Monty. He's a good guy. He takes numbers on the side. Races, too. Sort of like a mobile OTB."

"Sounds like a king among men," Claire grumbled as she took the card. "I'm going to get in touch with him and try to buy the car back."

275

"But it's worth so much! How will you afford it?"

"How will I afford it? How the hell should I know?" She turned to leave, then faced him one more time. "You sure picked a funny time to worry about how I can afford things, Dad."

"Where are you going?"

"I don't know." She breathed in and let it out in a rush. "Home, I guess." She pointed at him. "You're not leaving this property, do you hear me? And if you pull anything before I straighten this out you're on your own."

She didn't wait for his apology or his explanation this time. She stomped down the steps and got back behind the wheel of her very practical, very boring Prius. She turned the ignition and faced the car back toward Cypress Corners.

And cried the whole way home.

***

Jake ached all over, but he felt pretty damn good. Nearly all the infrastructure was ready and the finish grading would be done by midweek. Then the equipment could be installed the next week and assembly would fly.

He knew how this worked. The slow part was just about finished and soon he'd be testing the courses and making sure they were safe. And having a blast while he was doing it.

He took a shower as the sun was starting to set, then pulled on a clean pair of jeans and a long-sleeved T. Harmony was a doll to let him do his laundry at their house, and he took her up on it a couple of times a week. He grabbed up his dirty work clothes and shoved them in his laundry duffle, planning on toting it along when he stopped by to visit Rick and the family tomorrow. Tonight was Saturday night though, and he had one thought on his mind at the moment. Claire.

It had been weird this morning. She'd been her usual self. Not demanding or whiney or anything. Yet he'd felt himself pushing her away even as she was obviously trying to ease his worries about the project. He'd stopped just short of being a prick, but barely. Now that he felt better about the progress he'd made, and that his rotten dinner with Bill and Tiffany was a little further in the past, he could concentrate on what he and Claire were good at: making each other feel good and leaving the

277

emotional stuff out of it.

He thought about her at odd times, though. Thought about her both in and out of bed. She was funny and sweet. She was strong and determined. She was caring and a good friend. He never had woman friends. She'd hit the nail on the head with that one. She felt like a friend, though.

She'd listened to him when he talked about his mother and what she went through after Bill left them. She'd sat through dinner with his nightmare of a father and stepmother and lived to tell the tale. He would just admit to himself that he liked hanging out with her. He'd leave the rest of it alone. He was leaving soon anyway.

When he got to Claire's house he saw the Prius parked at the curb. He was sure she'd drive the T-bird back from her dad's today. She loved that car and looked so damn hot in it. Getting out of the Jeep, he walked up to her front door and rang the bell. Then rang it again.

Nothing. There was a light on inside. Through the frosted glass he could see it and figured it was one of the table lamps in the living room. He knocked on the door then.

"Claire?"

He heard a muffled reply from inside, then a click as she threw the lock on the door. She didn't open it.

"It's open."

Turning the knob, he opened the door. She'd retreated to the couch, curled up on one side.

"What's wrong? Are you sick?"

"No." Her voice was flat and thick.

He studied her. She was in her pajamas and, from the rumpled look of them, she'd been in them all day.

"Did you go see your dad today?"

She lifted her head a little, then gave a harsh laugh. "Oh, yeah. I saw him."

He had no idea what was wrong, but something definitely was. Sitting down near her feet, he placed a hand on her leg. "Claire, what's going on?"

"What's going on," she repeated. "Hmm." Coming to a seated position, she scrubbed her hands over her face and turned to him. "My father lost it."

He shook his head. In the dim light he could see that she'd been crying. Her hair was in a tangled ponytail and her eyes looked a little puffy. "Lost it?"

"Yep." She sniffed and folded her legs under her. "He gambled with it and lost it."

"What?"

"The car, Jake. He lost the Thunderbird." She swallowed audibly. "My Thunderbird. And for what he owes the guy who has it now, I don't know if I can ever buy it back."

Jake's heart broke for her. There was something more here, though. More than just a car. "What happened, baby?"

She took in a shuddering breath. "Reality, Jake. Reality bit me hard on the butt today and I can't ignore it any longer."

"What reality?"

"My dad is an addict. A gambling addict, but an addict just the same."

Her words didn't make sense but he guessed this had happened before. Often enough that she scrimped and saved and handled everything for her father.

"But you'll get it back. I know it."

"Oh, I will. It will take a huge chunk of my savings and put a big damper on my Christmas, but what am I going to do?"

Jake went to wrap his arms around her but she pulled away.

"Don't."

"Why not?" Jake stroked her arm. "I want to make you feel better."

She faced him, her eyes so very sad he felt it in his gut.

"You can't. I have to do this myself. Like I've always done. Like I always will."

A coldness settled over him. "What are you saying?"

"This," she waved a hand between them. "This is over, Jake. Whatever fun we were having, I just don't have the luxury of indulging myself any longer."

"Now, wait a minute."

"No. You're leaving in a couple of weeks anyway. Why put off the inevitable?"

His mouth fell open. "Because I like being with you. And you like being with me."

A half-smile lifted a corner of her mouth. "Yeah, I do. But I was a fool to think it was anything more than that."

"More than what?"

"More than scratching an itch, Jake. I got distracted by the hot guy wanting me for once. I threw my usual caution to the wind. Like an idiot."

"You're not an idiot. You're the smartest woman I know."

"Yeah, yeah. The money mind of Cypress. That's me."

That flat tone was back in her voice. "That's not what I meant."

"Look, Jake. It's been fun." That smile was back but it was sadder still. "A lot of fun. But it's over."

He sat there like he'd fallen off a bridge without a bungee. "You're serious."

"Dead serious. I'm sorry."

Just like that, the door slammed shut on whatever this was between them. Now there was nothing but cordiality and a polite good bye.

He came to his feet. "Okay." He didn't have to be told twice. Okay, he did but maybe not more than twice. "I'll go. You know how to reach me."

"For a booty call? Nope. Not going to happen."

He reached the front door and faced her. "Why not?" he had to know.

"Because if I'm going to quit you I have to do it cold turkey."

He guessed that was something. He'd have a damn hard time quitting her. That was for sure.

Chapter 22

"Damn it!" Jake growled and threw the tangled harness to the ground.

"Easy, bro."

He whipped his head around to see Rick walking toward him. His brother appeared casual but Jake saw the concern on his face.

"I'm just having a little trouble with this harness."

"Yeah?" Rick came closer and reached down to pick up the mass of straps and webbing. "Is it not to your specs?"

Jake blew out a breath and nodded. "Yeah, it's to my specs. I just can't get the damn thing untangled."

Rick made a show of looking at the equipment arrayed on the crates. "How's the rest of the stuff?"

"Fine," Jake snapped. He immediately cooled. "Sorry, Rick. This has been a bitch trying to get everything ready early."

"Ready for what? The official opening isn't until the end of the year."

Jake nodded. "I know, but I wanted to get this thing up and running faster than that."

"Why?"

The question hung in the air between the brothers but Jake kept his mouth shut tight. A realization dawned in Rick's eyes, though. And it just pissed Jake off all the more.

"God, tell me you're not killing yourself for Bill."

Jake cursed and stalked into the shed that would serve as a base of operations. The computers had yet to arrive and there were boxes of brochures and equipment everywhere in here, but he didn't see it. He just envisioned it as he wanted it to be. Finished and buzzing with activity.

Rick followed him and Jake was grateful they were alone for the time being. His big brother was going to lay something big on him and Jake was in no mood for an audience when he told him to fuck off.

"Don't do this, man," Rick said. "Don't try to please that son-of-a-bitch."

"Don't tell me what to do."

The words were biting but they lacked the force Jake had hoped for. Rick didn't even flinch.

"I know his games. Did he challenge you? Tell you

there was no way you'd meet the deadline for the opening? He's playing mind games, Jake. Like he always does."

Jake settled back against the counter and crossed his arms, hoping he looked a little more relaxed than he felt. There was a bunch of bees buzzing in his head, rapidly moving to his stomach. He wouldn't let his brother see that, though.

"This has nothing to do with Bill."

When Rick raised a brow, Jake cursed again. "All right, it has a little bit to do with Bill. But it's on me, Rick. I'm the one who wants to get this thing open and running."

"To prove to him that you can do it? Shit, you don't have to prove anything to him."

Jake pulled his gaze away from his brother's. "That's easy for you to say. You got the hell out of there."

"And I couldn't be a happier man."

Jake shrugged off his brother's words, but he didn't need them to know Rick was a damn sight happier with his life now.

"Yeah well, I don't have a loving woman and an amazing kid. You have every reason to be happy."

"And you're just a poor guy who can bed any woman he wants. I'm crying for you."

"Not any woman I want."

Jake bit his tongue but the words were out there now. He heard Rick take a few more steps toward him but couldn't look him in the face.

"You miss her."

"Who?" Jake asked as he faced Rick. "Claire? Hey, she's the one who ended it. We were just having fun anyway."

"If you say so."

"She said so, man. Not me."

"And did you argue with her?"

"What the hell for? I wasn't going to convince her to keep up our couch calisthenics until I left for good."

"Couch what?"

Jake waved a hand. "Never mind. What we had was good but now it's over. It's what she wanted and I'm fine with it."

"Yeah, you look fine."

287

"Maybe I just need to get laid."

Rick gave him a half-smile. "If you say so."

"Stop saying that," Jake growled. "Now if you're finished, Mr. Lonely Hearts, I have work to do ."

Rick pulled back at his outburst, but shrugged in that easy-but-not-so-easy way he had and turned to go. "The courses look great, by the way."

"Thanks. I'm going to test out some of the apparatus this week."

Rick turned with a jerk. "So soon? Have they been inspected?"

"The inspections will come when the courses are complete. I just want to try out some of the bridges and running trails. Maybe climb a wall or two."

"Be careful, man. You're my only brother."

Now Jake gave him a wide grin. "Hey, don't worry about me. I have nine lives."

Rick snorted and walked out of the shed. "Well then maybe you should trying living one of them like a grownup."

Jake flipped him the finger even though he knew Rick wouldn't see it. He slammed his hand down on the counter and went back outside to sort through the harnesses.

Maybe he'd go for a hard run through the wilder parts of the courses. That would burn up some energy and help clear his mind. He missed Claire, but he wasn't going to admit that to his brother. It was bad enough that when they'd been dating Rick and Harmony had practically hummed the wedding march every time they went over to their house. It wasn't what Claire wanted. No. That wasn't why she kicked him out of her bed. He could guess the real reason.

He wasn't worth the trouble of trying to work out whatever they had. He was a good lay. He was a good time. It was what he always shot for and he'd hit the target big time with the pretty redhead. If he missed the talks and the laughs, that was just his too bad. He'd find another girl to share more than sex with.

It didn't escape him that he'd never found one before Claire, though.

"Mr. Chapman, did you need something?" Jim, one of the construction guys, asked him.

"What?" Jake saw that Jim stood over near one of

the smaller climbing walls. A warm-up wall, set not far from the shed and meant to give visitors a taste before committing to the adventure. "No, man. Just thinking."

Jim nodded and looked over at one of the bridges stretching across the other side of the lake. Jake followed his gaze. The bridge was thirty feet above the lake and, if the weather was bad, they'd have to close down that portion.

"Have you run the bridges yet?" Jim asked.

Jake shook his head. "No, man. Not yet, but I'm dying to."

Jim laughed. "Dying is right. You'd never get me up there."

"Ah, come on." Jake grinned at him. "It's only thirty feet."

"Yeah. Thirty feet over rough terrain or the lake full of gators."

"Animal control is going to check for alligators."

"Still. No way I'm going up there."

"I can't wait to give it a go."

Jim just chuckled and went back to checking the braces on the climbing wall. Jake knew this course by heart and that bridge fell right at the three mile marker. Not too far into the run that a participant might be too winded to make it across yet still far enough to challenge them if they weren't used to the physical test.

It looked graceful and smooth, and it was. For the most part. It also swayed with the number of other runners making their way across and the movement became more marked during a heavily-participated race. Jake had emails from several obstacle-running clubs who wanted to be among the first groups to try it out but Jake couldn't risk signing off on anyone giving it a go just yet. Not until he himself tried every nook and cranny of this course and made sure it was safe.

After all, he knew just how to make it more of a challenge for a guy like himself. A guy who threw himself into the risk for the thrill of it.

With Claire out of his bed and out of his life, it seemed like that was all the thrill he was going to get until he got the hell out of Cypress Corners.

***

Claire dragged herself out of bed on yet another lonely Sunday. More than two weeks had passed since her world had blown apart. Two hectic, hellish weeks during which she'd done everything she could to secure the money to start to pay the guy back for the Thunderbird. More than once she'd told herself she was an idiot to be going so far out on a limb for a car but it was more than that to her. It was everything.

Yes, it was the principle of the thing but it was more than that, too. It was her pretty little car and it held fond memories for her. Memories of her mom and dad when they were happier. Of her and Jake when she was taking things in the moment for once in her life. It was her damn car and she was going to get it back. What else did she have in her life anyway?

Tammy had asked her what was wrong again and again, until finally giving up and taking Claire at her word that everything was okay. She was really a good friend and never mentioned Jake or the fact that it was obvious she wasn't dating him anymore. Mr. Forbes had asked about Jake only once before Tammy put an end to that line of questioning with a swift change of subject. Another point in Tammy's favor.

Claire dreaded someone asking her outright just

what the heck had happened. She had no reason to give should someone ask her. She'd given up hot sex with a great guy for what? To soothe her ego? To keep herself safe? God, that last one was the straw to the camel's back for her.

She did do it to keep herself safe. Jake would leave. That was inevitable. Jake would give her many more orgasms if she'd kept him around until then. Maybe many more laughs too, if she hadn't ended it early. She knew herself, though. She knew her heart. If she'd kept up their relationship her heart would rip in two when he blithely left Cypress Corners to return to the next spot needing his particular genius for thrill-making.

It was three o'clock in the afternoon. About the time she usually checked in with Cally. She dreaded the call but she had to make it. It was up to her to keep the lines of communication open if she was ever going to sustain her relationship with her father. She still hadn't forgiven him. How could she? But she lacked the balls to cut him loose and, in her heart, she could never really do that. Not completely.

Grabbing her phone, she sank down onto the couch.

293

Tapping on her father's name on the screen, she stared at the pretty poppy orange lantern on the fireplace mantel.

"Hello," came Cally's chipper voice.

She stilled for a moment. Chipper. Not manic. That was good.

"Hi, Dad."

"Claire-bear! It's so good to hear from you."

Claire bit back the reminder that he heard from her every day now. She wasn't going to slip back into that lazy trust thing she'd had going when she was busy getting wrapped up in Jake Chapman. That was part of the risk he posed to her sanity if not her heart. No. Never her heart.

"How are you today, Dad?"

"Good, good. There was bingo in the rec center today but I didn't go."

Claire pushed aside the guilt that threatened to rise. She'd forbidden him from any activities remotely involving gambling. Call her a bitch, but she didn't care.

"I'm sorry you had to miss it, but—"

"But I had to, I know," Cally finished for her. "I miss you, too. I missed you yesterday."

It was the second Saturday in a row she'd
deliberately stayed away from him. Just the thought of
him making some excuse or trying to charm his way out
of the mess he'd given her turned her stomach. She
couldn't bear to put herself through it. And she couldn't
bear taking the risk that she'd cave like her mother
always did. Like she herself always did.

"We'll get together soon."

There was a beat of silence, then she heard him sigh.
"Do you promise?"

Those three words nearly ripped her heart out of her
chest. He sounded so small in that moment.

"Yes, Dad. I promise."

Another silence, longer this time, stretched between
them. Claire finally cleared her throat past the thickness
there and smiled even though he couldn't see it.

"What are you doing tonight, Dad?"

"They're showing a movie in the rec center. One of
the superhero flicks. Should be good."

"Yeah." She took a breath. "Should be good."

She stood and paced, unable to sit any longer.
"Okay, then. You have a good time. Don't forget to set

your pills up for this coming week."

"I will."

"Good. I'll call you tomorrow."

"Thanks, honey. I love you."

Now those three words were just what she needed to hear at the moment. More tears threatened but she fought those too.

"Love you, too," she pushed out.

She disconnected the call and closed her eyes. "Damn it, Dad. Why did I let you do this to me again?"

She could never ask him that straight out. He'd have no real answer. It was a part of who he was. Of what he was.

She was the one who'd been stupid enough to forget that and to try to have her own damn life for once.

Chapter 23

Jake breathed hard as he flew over the gravel, his heart pounding with every step. He'd run over eight miles so far and he had no intentions of stopping any time soon. The course was holding up well, though the only other divots in the path were those made by him on his earlier pass. The bridge had been a thrill at mile three and he couldn't wait to hit it again now that he had completed the 10K course once already and was giving it another go. Twice around would make the equivalent of a half-marathon and he wasn't so big a pussy that he couldn't manage that today.

A loud crack of thunder sounded over his head but he didn't break his pace. An autumn cold front was just what he needed this afternoon. Thanksgiving was next week and the pre-opening would coincide with the Winter Festival in the Town Center the first weekend of December. It was only right that he test it out himself now. It was what he'd worked so hard for the past few weeks, and he wasn't going to let bad weather get in the way of his good time.

As if mocking his conviction, rain began to fall with

297

a vengeance. Swiping at his eyes, he pressed on into the last curve right before the bridge. His shoes slipped on the gravel as he swiveled to turn and pain shot up his right leg. Cursing, he tamped down the discomfort and kept up, only slowing his pace a bit as he headed for the bridge up ahead.

The rain was driving down in sheets now, the sky billowed with gray clouds and resounding with claps of thunder. A sane man would call it quits. Take the easy way out and limp back home. But he wasn't a sane man. And he didn't have a home. He was Jake fucking Chapman, thrill-seeker and daredevil, or so he told himself. He would finish this damn circuit and then take a hot shower and fall into bed.

That's all he'd been doing since he'd last been with Claire. Working hard and working out and sleeping like the dead. It would almost be a relief to get back to Boston to touch base before ferreting out his next assignment.

Water puddled in front of the bridge as he jumped up to land on the wooden boards. His shoes slipped a little and his right ankle cursed him out. Grabbing on to the rope rigging on the railing on the right-hand side, he pulled himself along as he began to sprint across the bridge.

The wind had kicked up since the rain began, and the bridge swayed under the strain. He was out over the lake now, making quick progress toward the footing on the other side. As he crossed above he ran past the water and was out over the sandy soil at the lake's edge. Suddenly the bridge gave a lurch and he reached for the nearest rigging. The rope tore through his palm and he hissed out a breath as he pulled his hand away. The next second he started to slip and was soon airborne as the lakeshore rushed up to meet him.

Then the day went black.

***

Claire brooded in her office, staring out the window at the still-green trees getting drenched in the thunderstorm. The wind kicked up too, judging by the dance the leaves were doing across the soaked sidewalk. She was all caught up with her work. Her work at Cypress, anyway. She would have to start taking on private clients but she wouldn't see much money from that avenue until the first of the year when the tax season began. For now she would help people write up their own budgets and find ways to live within their means. Means. Hers were getting leaner and meaner as the time passed.

The clock inched toward three o'clock and she had to get up and stretch before she let the sound of the rain and wind lull her to sleep. Walking into the break room, she headed for the coffee maker. A stack of ceramic mugs sat nearby, so she grabbed one. As she turned the rack to choose a coffee pod, Mr. Forbes came in.

"Hello, Claire."

"Hello, Mr. Forbes." She popped the pod into the coffee maker. "Can I make you a cup?"

"No, thank you."

She pressed the button and as the machine brewed her coffee he didn't say anything more.

"I'll be out of here in a second," she said, pouring creamer and some sweetener into her the cup.

Mr. Forbes held up a hand. "I'd like to speak with you, if I may."

Claire came to a stop, holding her steaming coffee cup in her hand. "With me?"

"Yes. Can we go into your office?"

"Sure." She led the way to her office and set the mug on her desk. "What can I do for you, Mr. Forbes?"

He closed her door and waved her into her chair. "Sit, Claire."

She did, her stomach giving a little twirl. "Is this about my taking on other clients?"

"No, no. You're a CPA and entitled to take private clients." His brows rose. "As long as there will be no conflict of interest?"

"None, sir."

"Good. No, I want to talk to you about the pressure you've been under."

"Pressure?" She'd thought she'd managed to stay on an even keel through the mess that was her current life. "I'm not under pressure."

"You are." He held up a hand. "I don't mean to take away from your work, Claire. I have no worries where that's concerned. This is more about your personal life."

She bristled even as her cheeks grew hot. "That's personal, just as you said."

"I don't know why you stopped seeing Jake

301

Chapman and that's not what this is about. You've been putting yourself through the ringer and I don't believe it's because you're lovesick."

"No, it's not."

"Then what is it?"

"Nothing."

He tilted his head and fingered his neat mustache. "Come, now. Something is wrong and I believe it has been for several weeks now."

Her throat tightened and her eyes burned and she couldn't hold back a second longer.

"My father lost all our savings three years ago, including our house. We moved here and I've been taking care of his expenses and now he's gone and gambled away my beautiful Thunderbird and I'm doing everything I can to get it back."

The words had rushed out of her and she felt deflated after her tirade. Mr. Forbes just gazed at her, the expression on his face tender and fatherly.

"I knew it had to be something like that. Don't get me wrong, Claire. I love how dedicated you are to your job. How diligent. But I've always sensed there was something else going on." He pulled a tissue out of the box set on her bookcase and handed it to her. "And now with the added pressure you're putting on yourself? It's no wonder you look so sad."

"Sad?" She wiped at her eyes, dabbed her nose and thought for a moment, then shrugged. "No. The tiredness I can blame on my work and my father. The sadness? That's squarely on Jake's broad shoulders."

He shifted in his seat, looking a little uncomfortable now. "And that's my cue. I don't do the emotional stuff."

Claire managed a smile and waved the tissue at him. "Don't worry. I'll plug up the waterworks. I promise."

"You know, there's no shame is asking for help."

"I've always handled everything myself, Mr. Forbes. I can go on doing that."

"You can. That's true." He stood now and opened the door. "I'm just saying you don't have to. You have friends here. I like to think we have a little family of sorts here, too. My door is open if you need to talk."

"Thank you."

He smiled at her and she felt a bit of her strain lift. "Very well. Enough maudlin discussions for the day." He glanced out the window behind her. "Although it seems to fit the weather." He squinted. "Is that fire and rescue?"

Claire followed his gaze and watched as the trucks screamed by, their lights blurry through the rain-spattered window. "I wonder what's going on?"

"Shit!" Rick ran past her door, his phone pressed tight to his ear. "I'm on my way."

Claire and Mr. Forbes shared a look, then they both went out into the hall and followed Rick into the lobby.

"Rick, what's going on?" Claire asked.

He stopped, and she saw how ashen his face was. Her heart stopped for a second.

"Is it Nick?" she asked.

He blinked. "No. No, thank God. It's my idiot brother."

Tammy came out to stand next to Claire. "What happened?" she asked.

Rick ran a hand over his face. "He fell. Off the damn rope bridge. They're taking him to the emergency room."

Claire's breath left her body and she thanked God Tammy was there to lean against. "Is he okay?"

"I don't know. He wasn't conscious when they

found him but he woke up and had them call me. I have to go."

"Go," Tammy said. "Keep us posted."

Rick nodded and ran out into the rain as the fire and rescue trucks raced past them on their way out of Cypress.

"I hope he's okay," Mr. Forbes said. "What was he doing out on the course in this weather?"

Claire's breath was shallow as emotions crashed through her. Fear and regret and anger. Oh, yeah. She was so pissed at him right now.

"Because he's a thrill-seeker, Mr. Forbes." She went back to her office and grabbed her purse, and then she noticed how bad her hands were shaking.

"I'll drive you," Tammy said, touching her shoulder.

"Thank you." Claire pulled on her jacket and went out into the rain. "He better live long enough for me to tell him how big an asshole he is."

Tammy smiled but didn't say anything as she drove toward the hospital. When they arrived Tammy dropped her off in front of the big glass doors and Claire ran inside.

Her eyes darted around the waiting room, which wasn't too crowded. The nice thing about living near a small city was the small hospital. She hadn't missed the helipad right outside the emergency room though. She prayed Jake wouldn't have to be airlifted to Orlando. She ran up to the desk and the gray-haired woman seated behind eyed her.

"Can I help you?"

"Jake Chapman," Claire rushed out. "I think they just brought him in?"

"Are you a member of the family?"

"No."

"Then I can't tell you anything." The woman's gaze softened. "Have a seat. I'm sure the family will be out soon."

"Thank you."

"Claire!"

Claire turned to see Harmony hurrying in through the sliding doors. "Harmony."

"Rick called me." Harmony pressed a hand to her midsection. "I had Lettie run over to watch Nick. Have you heard anything?"

"I'm not family." God, had any lonelier words every been spoken? "I'm sure they'll let you in."

Harmony nodded and walked over to the desk.

Claire grabbed a magazine from the low table in front of her and tried to make sense of the words swimming on the page. It was only when a tear dropped on the paper that she realized she was crying.

"Claire, I'm going in."

Claire wiped her eyes and looked up at her friend. "Okay."

Harmony reached out to touch her hand. "I'll be out soon to let you know what's going on. I promise."

Claire nodded. Tammy came in, shaking out her umbrella as she walked over. "Any word?"

"Nope."

"I'll sit with you." Tammy settled next to her on another vinyl chair and stared up at the TV set up in one corner.

"Thanks."

Claire couldn't seem to hold onto a thought. She was so nervous and worried and pissed off she could hardly think, really. Time seemed to drag as she waited for

Harmony to return. When she checked her phone she saw
that twenty minutes had passed, though it felt like twenty
hours.

"Hey," Tammy said softly, giving her a nudge.

Claire looked over and Tammy tilted her head
toward the desk. Rick stood there, his hands braced on
the counter as he spoke to the receptionist.

"Does he look worried?" Claire asked Tammy.

"A little. Not terrified, though."

"That's good, right?"

"Sure." Tammy crossed her legs and nodded. "Sure,
it is."

Rick smiled at the woman, then walked over to
Claire. "Come on."

Claire gaped up at him. "I'm not family."

"I am, and the nice lady at the desk says that you can
come in with me."

Rising slowly to her feet, Claire let Tammy take the
magazine from her limp fingers and followed Rick
through swinging wood doors and down the wide white
hallway to a small room set off to the right.

She heard Harmony's voice from inside, but couldn't

make out the words. As she stepped into the room, she gasped as she saw how banged up Jake was. He was wearing one of those cotton gowns with the dots or whatever on it and his face and arms were scratched all over. His hair was caked with sand and he looked pale. He never looked better to her.

"Jake!" Her feet flew as she ran toward the bed. She stopped, gripping the side rail. "You're okay. Are you okay?"

Jake nodded, managing a small smile. "They think I broke my foot but, yeah, I'm okay."

She saw then that his right leg was elevated and thick bandaging wrapped his foot and ankle.

"They took an X-ray, so we'll know more soon," Rick said.

"You were unconscious," Claire remembered Rick had said. "What happened?"

"I went out for a run on the course."

"In this weather?" she asked.

He shrugged. "It wasn't raining when I started out."

Anger simmered in her belly. "But it was before you finished, wasn't it?"

309

He shrugged again and she lost it.

"What the hell is wrong with you? I know you don't give a shit about yourself but what about your family? What about the people who love you?"

Jake opened his mouth but evidently she wasn't done.

"You take these risks for, I don't know, the thrill of it with no thought to the people who would die if they lost you. You just had to go up there and test the course before it's ready. You just had to go out there to prove something to your frigging father, like he's ever going to acknowledge what you're capable of."

"Claire, wait," Jake began.

She held up a hand. "I can't do this. I can't be with someone with so little regard for his life and the lives of the people who love him. So go! Finish your damn project and go back to Boston. Go to Europe. Go to the four corners of the world, if you want to. Just go, because that's what you're good at."

With that parting shot, she stormed back out into the waiting room. Her breath came fast and her pulse raced but she'd said her piece.

When Tammy wrapped her arms around her, she let the tears come again.

Chapter 24

Jake rested on the couch at Rick and Harmony's, watching some robot cartoon show Nick had left on before he went to play in his room. Jake's foot was set and his cuts were healing. He hadn't even had to stay overnight at the hospital, but he still felt like he'd been zip-lined and run over by a herd of cattle. They'd confirmed three fractures in his foot but his rock-hard head was fine. He couldn't get Claire's words out of it, though.

She'd looked so frightened when she'd rushed into that room. Her face had been sweet and dear and concerned. And then she'd let loose like Mussolini from the balcony. Her words had cut him worse than any fall from an obstacle could. Two days after his fall, and he still felt like he was on that swinging bridge.

"How's the foot?"

He glanced up at his brother, who was just coming in from work. "Can't kick."

Rick's face broke into a smile. "Funny. Head still hurt?"

"Not too much. Harmony's been making sure I take

my meds."

Rick nodded as he set his keys on the counter. "So what are you going to do about it?"

"About what?"

His brother snorted and came to sit on the chair next to the couch. "Seriously? About the situation with Claire."

"There is no situation with Claire."

"Right."

"You heard her, bro. You heard the things she said. She doesn't want to have anything to do with me."

Rick stared at him for a beat. "Oh my God, you're so stupid."

Jake frowned. "What are you talking about? She told me to go, Rick. To get the hell away from her."

"Did you hear the other things she said? How you don't have any regard for the people who love you?"

"Yeah, so?" Realization dawned on him like the sunrise on their last morning together. "I'm an idiot."

"Yep."

Jake stared at his brother. "Do you really think she loves me?"

"Yes, though I have to wonder if you're too stupid to love her back."

Jake's smile made his lip split a little but he couldn't keep it in. "No way, bro. I'm not that stupid."

"Good." Rick grabbed the remote and started flipping through the channels. "Maybe another Chapman has a chance at this happiness stuff. It's pretty awesome, by the way."

"Yeah," Jake answered.

But his mind was on Claire and on just how he could show her he wanted what they had to last forever.

***

Claire turned off her computer and sat back. Another week's work done. She'd thought a lot about Mr. Forbes' words on the afternoon of Jake's accident two weeks ago, and was trying to secure a loan to get the car back. She really didn't want to stretch herself so thin by taking on private clients through the tax season. It was mind-breaking work and it was bad enough she was facing a long lonely winter. She shouldn't have to face it wiped out too.

Friday night. Tomorrow was the day she'd thought

to go to Cally's. At least for a short visit. She couldn't keep freezing him out. She just wasn't built that way. She'd proved that to Jake and his family on that horrible night in the emergency room.

God, she'd carried on like a crazy person. She hadn't heard from Jake since, but that wasn't surprising. He'd never contacted her after she'd ended things. Why would he now that she'd practically ripped him a new one?

Rick had since told her that Jake had stayed at their house for a few days before going back out to the tent-cabin just the other day. He had a walking cast and the doctors expected him to have no lasting effects from his accident.

"Accident," she grumbled. "Deliberate daredevil baloney, was more like it."

Claire gathered her things and stepped outside to get into her car. A lovely autumn evening promised her a nice brood on the front porch as she contemplated what she was going to do with the rest of her life.

As she pulled up to her house her mouth fell open. There at the curb, resting in all its loveliness, was the Thunderbird.

"What the heck?" she murmured.

She stopped her car and stepped out, gaping at the car. It glistened in the soft light of the sunset and she reached out a hand to caress its rear fender. How did it get here? She hadn't yet secured payment to get it back from the collector.

"It's yours, Claire."

She jumped at the sound of Jake's voice. He stood on her porch, leaning against the post and resting his plastic-booted foot on the step.

"What did you say?"

"It's yours. I got it back for you."

"I... You what? This isn't..." Words slammed together in her head but she couldn't seem to form a coherent sentence. "I don't get it."

Jake thumped down the steps and walked toward her, swinging his injured foot as he came. She saw little evidence of his accident other than the boot. His cuts and bruises looked like they were pretty much healed. He looked at gorgeous as ever, with that light stubble on his cheeks and those eyes of his.

"I'm not going anywhere," he said. "Not to Boston.

Not to Europe. I'm staying here."

She looked at the car again, then back at Jake. "What are you saying?"

"I'm saying I want this."

She blinked. "My car?"

He laughed, his eyes sparkling now. "No. I want what we have. I want to be with you."

His words stunned her. She stood stock still as he came up and wrapped his arms around her. In the next second she melted against him with a sigh. Oh, she could smell him. "Do you mean it?"

He kissed her temple. "Yes. I love you, too."

"Hmm." She pulled back to peer up at him. "You love me? Too?"

"Yes." He touched her face and smiled wider. "I remembered what you said when you were yelling at me, Claire. You love me."

She thought to deny it, then she laughed. "I do."

He kissed her lips and she moaned softly as she tasted him again. How she'd missed him!

Pushing gently, she held him at arms' length. "But how did you know about the car?"

317

"Mr. Forbes told me."

She groaned. "He told you? When?"

"When I asked him if he knew what I could do to win you back."

"Oh my God, you asked him that?"

"Yep. Seems he's quite the romantic. Who knew?"

"But how did you know where it was?"

He turned her and started walking her toward the house. "I went to see your father."

Shame burned in her cheeks. "Cally. You went to see Cally?"

"He loves you, Claire. He's made a ton of mistakes but he loves you." Jake smiled again, stopping to take her hands in his. "Almost as much as I do."

"Well, I have to pay you back for the car."

"You don't. Consider it a wedding present."

She laughed. "Right."

She continued up the steps but when he wasn't beside her she turned back. "Do you need help up the stairs?"

"No."

"Then why are you standing there?"

"Because I can't get down on one knee with this damn boot on my foot."

"Down on one knee?" Her hand flew up to her chest and she gasped. "Oh."

"Marry me, Claire? I promise I won't put myself at risk again." He winked. "At too much of a risk, anyway."

She ran back to him and threw herself into his arms, only easing her hold when she felt him teetering a little. "Yes, I'll marry you. I love you."

"Good." He held her close. "Now let's get inside."

"The climax couch?" she asked in a whisper.

Jake laughed that low, sexy laugh and the two of them went inside.

Epilogue

Jake sat back from his desk, rubbing his eyes. He was still getting used to doing so much of his work at the computer but it was gratifying to see how successful the adventure courses had proven to be. Corporate clients, residents and locals all loved them and came back again and again. Athletes training for triathlons came too, using the many existing bike trails and finishing with the obstacle courses and swimming.

He was in charge of all the recreation at Cypress now, actually. And the place was getting buzz all over the place that it was a perfect setting to test your limits and then relax them away.

He was the one in charge of the kids' excursions, too. That was the most fun. Teaching kids how to stay safe while letting go was the best. He'd even promised Nick that they'd have a superhero kids' event in a few months. The fall would be a perfect time for it. The work was as fulfilling and he loved it. Staying here had been the best choice he'd ever made, and if he needed more evidence there she was standing in his doorway.

"Hey, there," he said, unable to keep a smile from

his lips.

Claire smiled back at him and walked in. "Ready to go home?"

Jake rubbed his eyes and stood. "Yep. The only thing that makes working here in the office worthwhile is the fact that I get to take home the money mind." He winked. "I get to take her to bed, too."

Her cheeks turned that sweet shade of pink he loved. "We're going over to your brother's tonight."

"Right. I forgot." He wrapped his arm around her shoulder and kissed her right on her mouth. "Come on. Drive me home."

She jingled her keys, now sporting a custom T-bird key ring he'd had made for her. "At your command."

They stepped out into the warm spring evening and got into the Thunderbird to drive to the house they now shared. They'd decided to live in her place after the wedding, which they'd celebrated right at the lakeside near the tent-cabin. They'd had their honeymoon there, too. Far from everyone and everything. It was the most fun Jake had ever had without risking his neck.

"Have you heard from your sister?" she asked as

they pulled up in front of their house.

"Nope. You saw the card she sent after the wedding, but that's it. Rick doesn't know where she is, either."

"Your father called again?"

"Yeah. Spoke to Mr. Forbes first, though. Typical Bill. Thinks he can talk anyone into anything if he waves around enough money."

She placed her hand on his and he unclenched the fist he hadn't known he'd made. "Mr. Forbes won't give you up, Jake. He wants you to work here at Cypress. He values you and you're the best Recreation Director we could hope to have."

He shrugged and got out of the car, going around to open her door as he always did. "You're biased."

She smiled and wrapped her arms around his neck. "I am." Kissing him, she took his hand. "I think we might have just enough time before we have to go over to your brother's."

Jake's heart raced and it was with anticipation instead of adrenaline. After he drove them both crazy on their favorite piece of furniture, he held her close.

"I love you, Claire. Always."

It was what he'd started saying after their reconciliation and he said it still.

"I love you, Jake. Always."

He breathed in her sweet scent and knew this was it. Better than the high dive. Better than a climb up a craggy side of a mountain. This was what he craved now. Not thrills and risks. Love and life.

Claire took her own chances with him, giving him her heart. He was damned if he'd let anything happen to it. For him, love was the biggest risk of all.

And he was damn glad he took it.

About the Author

JoMarie DeGioia has been making up stories for as long as she can remember, and has spent years giving voice to the characters in her head. She's known Mickey Mouse from the "inside," has been a copyeditor for her town's newspaper, and a bookseller. She writes Historical and Contemporary Romances, along with Young and New Adult Fantasy stories. She divides her time between Central Florida and New England.

Discover books by JoMarie DeGioia

The Dashing Nobles series, including

More Than Passion

Pride and Fire

Just Perfect

More Than Charming

The Cypress Corners series, including

Finding Harmony

The Gifted YA Fantasy/Adventure Trilogy,

including Gifted

Connect with me online

Twitter: https://twitter.com/JoMarieDeGioia

Facebook:

https://www.facebook.com/JoMarie.DeGioia.Author

Website: www.jomariedegioia.com

www.ingramcontent.com/pod-product-compliance
Lightning Source LLC
Chambersburg PA
CBHW070647180626
46817CB00006B/2271